B E   R

TERENCE MUNSEY

EMERALD
CITY

MUNSEY MUSIC
Toronto Los Angeles London

EMERALD CITY

published by:

MUNSEY MUSIC

Box 511, Richmond Hill, Ontario, Canada, L4C 4Y8

Fax: 905 737 0208

E-MAIL: munsey@pathcom.com

WEBSITE: www.pathcom.com/~munsey

Canadian Cataloguing in Publication Data

Munsey, Terence, 1953-

    Emerald city

ISBN 0-9697066-6-9

I. Title.

PS8576.U5753E43 1998   C813'.54   C98-930248-2

PR9199.3.M86E43 1998

Library of Congress Catalogue Number 98-65102

First MUNSEY MUSIC original soft cover printing April1998
Second printing August 1999

Cover design, and photograph © 1998 by TERENCE MUNSEY

Back cover photo taken by T. Goulding

Manufactured in Canada

Acknowledgments

A very special thank you to **Alison Kipp** for her proof reading of the early manuscript, and **Cindy Goldrick** for her many hours, comments and suggestions on the final manuscript. I truly appreciate the time you took to read and re-read the manuscripts.

Thanks to Shirley Dudgeon for the coffee and conversation.

And… Lady D.

Author's Note

EMERALD CITY is the second book in what is rapidly becoming the Monika Queller mystery series. I have come to look forward each year to the trips that Monika takes me on, and it is a pleasure to continue writing about them.

The next book, DIVE MASTER—set in South Florida and the Keys, is very thrilling. I hope you are enjoying reading the books as much as I enjoy writing them.

Terence

Open the curtain that keeps out the light.

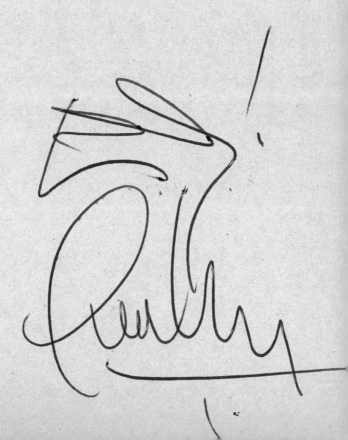

●

The sound of modems connecting can be heard in the darkened room. Gradually the light of a computer monitor comes into view. Upon the screen can be seen dialogue boxes as the modem is connecting and then downloading data from another computer. The other computer is in a federal department in Washington DC. There has been no security alert or password requested. It has been a very easy and straight forward operation. The computer is connected without problems and begins to give up its secrets.

●

Prologue

A late model General Motors grey sedan signaled. It had been traveling along the inside lane of the highway and was preparing to exit. Gradually it pulled off the highway and turned onto Eglinton Avenue heading westward. After several minutes the car crossed through a set of lights and continued along the road which began to rapidly slope downward. Off to the right were two tall buildings linked together and separated from the road by a plush green lawn. The two buildings had been recently renovated—where one hotel had previously stood occupying both buildings, now there were two separate hotels.

Halfway up the lawn from the road and the

hotels was a long stone wall about eight feet high. The wall helped to support the second tier of a large, gently sloping, meticulously manicured grass terrace which fronted one of the hotels. The hotels were both situated on the higher ground to the north of the road. The names of the hotels were written in large white letters on the wall.

Looking upward from the wall there were large signs, one on each hotel building at the topmost floor, which identified each structure: The Holiday Hotel and The Inn at the Park.

It was a picturesque location amidst the busy corporate world of the north end of Emerald City. Trees were densely scattered throughout the valley that the hotels bordered. The valley separated them from the surrounding high-rise condominiums and office complexes. The hotels' perch atop the long sloping lawns gave them the appearance of impregnable castles overlooking and dominating the treed natural valley below.

To the southwest could be seen the CN Tower pricking into the clear blue sky, closely surrounded by half a dozen majestic skyscrapers. It was a peaceful day and not much traffic was on the roads around the hotels.

The car's turn signal flashed. Once the traffic allowed, the car pulled off the main roadway and onto the side street that led towards the hotel. Fifty feet from the main intersection, the car slowly turned right onto the driveway to the hotels. Picking up speed, the car began its climb up the driveway to the lobby entrance of the Holiday Hotel.

The beautiful green lawn of the hotels' property gave way to reveal the cream-colored cement walls of the buildings as the car gradually rose to the level of the first building. The hotel building was not new, but a recent coat of paint freshened its appearance.

An outgoing taxi cab leaving with its fare passed by as the car approached the sign which gave directions to the two hotels. To the left was the Holiday Hotel main lobby and straight ahead the Inn at the Park. The car turned left and continued toward the Holiday Hotel lobby and parking area.

Over the driveway, at the entrance to the lobby, the second story of the Holiday Hotel was canopied, protecting new arrivals from the natural elements of the weather. Thousands of little lights embedded in the canopy roof illuminated the driveway and cast a glittering light.

Several feet before the main lobby entrance, three cabs were lined up and waiting. The grey sedan pulled up and around the first cab, stopping a few yards in front of the glass doors of the main lobby entrance. The driver's side door opened and a man wearing a dark business suit got out. He was in his early fifties, heavy set, with a neatly groomed balding black hairline. After closing the car door, the man checked his appearance in the reflection of the driver's side door window. He quickly adjusted his tie and pulled the lapels of his jacket to straighten and tidy up his look. Satisfied, he walked around the back of the car and stepped from the driveway to the sidewalk en route to the lobby entrance. As he neared the glass doors he waved off a doorman.

"I'll be a couple of minutes. Okay?" This was spoken in a pleasant accent not American nor British—it was Canadian. By the manner in which he announced to the doorman his intentions, it was obvious that he was on some sort of delivery or pick up.

Since the hotel wasn't very busy, the doorman nodded his consent for the car to be parked temporarily by the entrance.

The man turned and walked up to the main revolving doors. He briefly paused and looked into the hotel lobby. The glass doors gave a complete view of the space within. The man seemed to be expecting or looking for someone. He seemed a little uneasy. Before he continued in, he turned his head around and checked the outside area. Comfortable with his surroundings, he stepped into the revolving door then into the lobby.

Before him was a plushly decorated large area. The floor was covered with broadloom with a Persian-style pattern composed of red tones. To his immediate left was a large sitting area. Large high-backed Queen Anne chairs and settees were carefully placed throughout the room around small coffee tables, which appeared to be made out of a dark mahogany. There was a large hearth and fireplace on the north wall. The room in its richness was inviting and looked comfortable.

Straight ahead, about twenty feet from the revolving doors of the lobby entrance, was a wall of glass which overlooked a very tidy Japanese-style garden and outer courtyard. The green of the shrubs and trees softened the light as it found its way through this natural scene and into the lobby.

In front of the windows there was a staircase that connected the lobby to the second floor mez-zanine above. The stairs were about ten feet wide and ran up from right to left. The rise of the steps was not steep. The staircase added an impression of elegance to the room.

To his right, running at a slight angle to the rest of the area so as to give a clear view of the sitting area, entrance and garden, was the front desk. It was the only part of the room that did not fit in with the decor. There was a long highly polished cream-colored countertop which separated the elegance of the lobby area from the brightly lit efficiency of the business side of the hotel opera-tion. Behind this area was a man neatly dressed in a maroon jacket that was obviously the hotel uni-form. The employee had not yet noticed this new patron and was busy checking something on a small computer screen situated on the countertop to his right.

There was no one else in the room. The man crossed through the lobby area and made his way directly to the front desk.

"Good morning," he said to the employee as he came up to and stopped in front of him. The employee immediately looked up, and with a very pleasant smile, began his trained routine:

"Good morning Sir. Welcome to the Holiday Hotel. How may I help you?"

The man pulled out a small white card. Upon it, in simple black lettering, was written: 'Allied Services', a 1-888 phone number and the name Ted Ambrose. He presented it to the clerk as he asked, "Mr. Rosen, please."

The clerk looked at the card and then at the man and nodded.

"Right away, Mr. Ambrose. Mr. Rosen is expecting you. I'll let him know you're here. Excuse me a moment, please."

Mr. Ambrose seemed satisfied. The clerk picked up the phone at his front desk station, pushed an extension number, and awaited an answer. After what must have been ten rings the clerk spoke into the phone.

"Mr. Ambrose is here." After hearing the response he hung up the phone and said to Mr. Ambrose, "He'll be right down."

"Thank you," Ambrose replied.

"You're welcome, Sir."

Mr. Ambrose turned away from the clerk and walked back into the sitting area of the main lobby. He picked up a complimentary newspaper from a coffee table. He sat down in one of the chairs facing the garden and staircase. It was going to be a long day. He had been assigned this job late last night. It was very unusual, but then his business was not the normal courier service. His company specialized in personal deliveries of 'special' packages. Packages that clients did not want sent through the normal ways. Ted had worked for Allied twelve years now. He had learnt a long time ago not to question the jobs, only to reliably provide his services.

The package today was to be delivered to Los Angeles by late tonight. He would be met at the airport there and then return home to Emerald City on the next flight. He was then going to take his annual two week vacation. He was looking forward to it. He and his son were going fishing up north. Since his wife had died eight years ago, he had started spending this special time away with his son, his only child. It gave him great solace. Even after his son had moved out to start his own life, they had continued their fishing trips. It was an opportunity to stay in touch and close. To be a family. As he sat he reminisced about a happier past.

"Mr. Ambrose?" A younger well-dressed man who was coming down the staircase called out.

Ted was startled out of his daydream. He put down the paper and looked up to the staircase where he saw the man descending towards the lobby. Ted rose up from his chair and walked to meet him at the bottom of the staircase.

"Yes. Good morning," Ted replied.

The younger man stepped onto the carpeted floor of the main lobby. Ted presented his right hand but, before they shook, the man placed a small valise upon a pedestaled table that was beside them both at the beginning of the staircase and its balustrade.

"Good morning, " he answered as they shook hands.

The man was very abrupt in his manner. He did not introduce himself but got straight to business. He seemed to Ted to be a little nervous. Ted could not explain this feeling, but noticed that the man's demeanor was strained and uncomfortable.

"If you would sign this." Ted was presented with the usual documentation.

"Of course."

Ted pulled out a pen from his inside jacket pocket and quickly signed at the spot indicated by the man. The man then placed the signed paper into his pocket and reached over for the valise.

The valise reminded Ted of a doctor's medical bag. The man took the bag and handed it into

Ted's left hand. Ted took the bag without question. As he grabbed hold of its handle, there was a sudden unexpected movement by the man and Ted felt a cold metal object being clasped around his left wrist.

"What the…?" he exclaimed as the bag was handcuffed to his wrist. Ted was alarmed. This had never happened to him before. There was a short heavy chrome-colored chain linking his cuffed wrist to the bag.

"Please. Don't be alarmed Mr. Ambrose. It's just a precaution."

"What about the key?" Ted was displeased with what he felt was an effrontery.

"When you are met at Los Angeles," was all the man replied.

"But…" Ted decided not to complain further. Though unusual and uncomfortable, it would only be for a few hours. When he returned from this trip, he would have harsh words with his boss.

"Have a nice trip Mr. Ambrose." The man smiled, turned and, without waiting for Ted to finish his sentence, went back up the stairs.

Ted grimaced. There was no point in getting upset. He placed the bag by his side and crossed through the lobby to the main entrance. The whole meeting had taken only moments. No one else, other than the front desk clerk, had been in the lobby to witness these events.

Once outside the hotel, Ted quickly made his

way over to and got into his car. It was a twenty minute drive to the airport. He would have plenty of time to get to the airport and catch his flight. After placing the bag on his left leg he started his car. The chain was very short and it would be awkward for him to drive, but there was nothing he could do about it. He pulled out from his parking place and drove back down the driveway he had come in by.

Ted turned his thoughts back to his earlier daydream and the vacation that awaited him after the completion of this job. He remembered the first time he had gone up north alone with his then teenage son. He recalled how his wife had been worried that the boy was not ready for that kind of adventure, but he had reassured her that everything would be fine. Even he had had private concerns, but it had been a lovely trip and since that time they had never missed this yearly excursion.

His thoughts strayed to memories of his wife. How happy they had been. How he had loved being married and a family man. Somehow it gave meaning to his existence. There had been much more purpose to his life then. After his wife had died there had been an emptiness. A void in his life that he had not been able to fill. It was as if part of him had also died and gone from him with her passing. He longed for the day when they would be reunited; when the emptiness would finally be filled. If it had not been for the existence of his son, he would have gone mad with despair. He missed the family years; the living together. Life had become very lonely for him. All he had was his work and these two weeks once a year. These two weeks made his whole year worth living. He was happy to have something to look forward to; something that would rekindle the happiness that had once been a normal part of his life and taken for granted. He happily anticipated the upcoming vacation with his son.

As he arrived at the airport, Ted's thoughts returned to his job. He focused his attention on maneuvering along the confusing roadways into the airport terminals. He followed the sign for 'Terminal Two' and soon found his way into the short-term parking lot for international departures. He drove into the covered parking area after having taken a ticket from the machine at its entryway, and found a parking space close to the exit to the departure level. Before he got out of the car he pulled an envelope out of his jacket pocket with his right hand. The envelope contained his tickets. He quickly checked them and then, satisfied, got out of the car, locked it and walked through the garage. He had no luggage. There was no need. He would be back by tomorrow on the next day's return flight. The only bag he carried was the one handcuffed to his wrist.

The airport departure area was busy. He crossed

the street and entered through sliding doors which automatically sensed his presence and opened before him. Once inside the terminal, Ted stopped and looked for the airline check-in counter. After a few orienting moments he saw the counter to his left. There was a long line, but this did not concern him. Allied always sent their 'packages' first class, not economy. There would be no lining up or waiting for him. There was always a special counter for first class travelers.

Ted made his way up to the first class counter. A pretty ticket agent was seated behind the counter.

"Good morning sir," she pleasantly greeted him.

"Good morning," Ted replied as he handed the package of his tickets to the woman.

"How many pieces of baggage sir?"

"None... oh, just one carry-on." Ted remembered the valise which he was keeping at his side. He was embarrassed at being handcuffed to it.

The woman did not question or react to his statement, but continued with her job.

"Mr. Ambrose," she said out loud as she punched his name into her computer terminal. "Yes. Here we are. The 12:45 PM to LAX?"

"Yes. That's right," Ted confirmed.

"Returning 2:10 PM tomorrow?"

"Yes, that's correct."

"First class isn't full. In fact there is only one other passenger today, so I can give you a place by yourself next to empty seats if you would like?"

"Yes, that would be nice."

"3A."

He wasn't sure if she was asking or telling.

"Thank you."

There was a short pause while the computer confirmed the seating arrangements and the printer spewed out a boarding pass with Ted's name and seating location typed on it.

"Here you go, Mr. Ambrose. Would you like a sticker for your bag?" The women leaned forward and smiled as she handed Ted his boarding pass and other documents.

"No thank you."

"You are boarding at Gate 12Y. There is a courtesy lounge for first class passengers. Please go through Immigration over there." The woman indicated the U.S. Customs area that was directly behind the airline check-in area.

"Great. Thank you." Ted took the pass from her and proceeded over to Immigration.

"Have a great flight and thank you for flying..."

Ted did not hear her last words. He had already turned away from her and was concentrating on clearing Customs. Though his company had special waivers and clearances for such border crossings, Ted had never been in this particular situation. Never had he been handcuffed to his 'package'. It made him uneasy and embarrassed. He wondered how he would explain the handcuffed valise to the Customs agent. He did not want to have to go through any more red tape than he needed to. He was anxious to get this job over and get back to Emerald City, and his vacation. This handcuffing would only complicate matters and slow him down. It would make him very conspicuous. He did not like to be placed in such a position without his permission. He again resolved to himself to give his boss an earful upon his return.

There were many other passengers in the immigration area. Ted took a place in front of what he felt was a friendlier looking U.S. Customs agent. The line moved quickly. He soon found himself standing behind the red line that was taped to the grey carpet in front of the agent, and next to be processed. Ted was beckoned forward by the agent.

The Customs agent was uniformed and seated beside a black rubber luggage conveyor belt. Ted walked up and gave the agent his passport and boarding pass as the agent demanded:

"Where were you born?"

"London," Ted answered.

"You're a Canadian?"

"Yes."

"Purpose in the United States?"

The agent was not looking at Ted, but had swiped his passport through his computer reader. In moments information that could not be seen by

Ted was displayed on the agent's screen.

"Business."

"Purpose of your trip?"

"Business."

"Are you bringing anything into the United States to be left behind?" The agent looked up and paid attention.

"No. I'm attending a meeting and returning tomorrow." Ted calmly answered.

Although he was used to this type of questioning, he still felt tense. He tried to conceal the chain and handcuff from the agent.

There was a pause. Ted thought that he would be asked about the valise, but the agent matter-of-factly said: "Okay."

Ted took back his documents from the agent and without saying another word walked away from the counter. He suddenly needed a drink.

He walked down the corridor that led from immigration to the departure gate. Ahead of him was a search station. The attendants would definitely notice the handcuffs. He got out his documents and identification.

"Good morning," he said as he came to the search technicians. "Can you search this…" Ted indicated the valise and the handcuffs, "…through the x-ray? I don't have the key."

"No key?" The technician was East Indian and spoke in a heavy accent.

"I'm a courier," Ted said privately to him.

The technician seemed to understand. He guided the bag into the x-ray machine and then pulled it back out. He then used a wand to check Ted's person and other than the blurting sound the wand made when it came near to the chain and handcuff, there was no other problem.

"That's fine sir. You may go."

"Thank you." Ted was surprised and relieved but did not question the technician's decision. He walked on.

Gate 12Y was a little farther along the corridor. Upon arriving there, Ted found the first class lounge, opened the door and walked in.

It was a cozy room with three large sofas placed around a large table. There was no one else in the room. It was obviously too early to get a drink. He went over to the nearest sofa and plunked himself down in its comfortable softness. He sat back, placing the bag with his hand stretched out upon the sofa. He leaned his head back into the sofa and closed his eyes. There were forty five minutes before the plane would begin boarding.

Ted had not closed his eyes long when the lounge door opened. This noise brought him out of his rest. He opened his eyes as a pretty woman in an airline uniform walked in. She was in her early thirties: red-headed and shapely. The skirt of her uniform was short and Ted noticed that she was rather sexy looking. She carried a tiny silver-colored purse.

"Good afternoon, sir. Looks like you're the only one in first class. Can I get you something?" She was very nice and willing to please.

"Yes, thank you. A rye and ginger."

"Certainly sir. Would you like ice?" she asked as she crossed the room to a bar area behind the sofa Ted was sitting upon.

"No thanks." Ted leaned forward and picked up a magazine that was upon the table in front of him as the woman went out of sight behind him and into the bar. He began to leaf through the magazine.

Behind him the woman got out a glass and prepared his drink. As she was doing this, she quietly opened her purse and pulled out a small gun which had a silencing device attached to its muzzle. She kept up a pleasant inane chatter as she carefully pulled out the gun and slowly aimed it at the back of Ted's head. Once ready she suddenly stopped talking and the room became very silent. Ted noticed this sudden silence and put down the magazine. He turned to see what had happened. As he turned he was shocked to see the woman pointing the gun at him. He saw the weapon and, without saying a word, understood what was about to occur. There was nothing he could do. He was a sitting target.

As he turned and visualized all these things there was a 'pop' sound. The woman fired one sole shot. Time slowed. Ted saw the gun and the finger of the woman as she pulled the trigger. The bullet came rushing out of the barrel and he felt the impact of it instantly breaking through his forehead. A small hole marked the center of his forehead. Blood spewed out. He was pushed back by the impact and lost consciousness. Everything went black.

Chapter 1

TWO WEEKS LATER

The room was dark but, through the billowing sheer curtains at the large bedroom windows, the glow of the full moon cast its illumination. Two figures on a large four poster bed that was covered in a light-colored sheet and comforter could be seen in the shadows. They were making love, and the sound of them pleasuring each other was audible.

At first the man kissed and caressed the woman, who was passionately responding to his kisses as he moved from her lips down her neck, which she offered more of to him at his touch, and then her breasts as he firmly directed them with his hand to his lips. The woman moaned and called out his name.

"Oh James. Don't stop." She was was enjoying his touch, the crescendo of her desire growing.

In response, James began to gently suckle on the nipple of her left breast. Monika writhed. A pleasurable sensation ran through her and increased her excitement. She called out from her physical rapture and wrapped her smooth legs around James' hard body. She could feel the roughness of his masculine physique and smell the tangy aroma of him. It aroused her more. She tasted his salty skin as she nipped gently at his shoulders. He rolled over to his right side as she became more dominant. The bed covers were draped over them.

James shifted to lie on his back and Monika positioned herself over top of him. She opened her legs and straddled him, directing him into her. She felt his firmness and sighed as she slowly opened and slid over his hardness. Waves of desire filled her. She threw her head back and began to rock back and forth, riding him.

Monika was becoming louder as she slowly approached her physical frenzy. A sense of urgency filled her as she built toward her climax. As she pumped, James caressed her breasts sending shocks of electricity to her core. The combination of these sensations made her lose control. She became more frantic and increased her motion as she strained to take in more and more of him. Her rational mind was no longer in control. She was now fully intoxicated by her arousal. She could sense the power of James' desire. She could feel his hard, pulsating warmth as he responded to her motion. She knew he was close and this excited her even more. She played with these sensations, trying to keep control over herself and James. It was such a good feeling. Her whole being was in love with him. She did not want these feelings or sensations ever to stop.

She felt a surge of emotion and a stronger wave of physical desire struck her. She cried out and fell forward. Her frenzy was now very strong and the waves of her arousal intensified. She felt James' taut chest against her hardened nipples. She began to kiss him as she rocked and pressed upon him. She moaned. She could no longer stop the inevitability of her passion. She could smell the sweet scent of their union.

She began to cry out, "Yes! Yes! Yes!"—and then there was a long pause as she felt the strongest wave of need and then his explosion within her. Her satisfaction was complete as she felt the sudden surge of warmth inside her. She kissed him.

"I love you," she whispered in a soft affectionate voice as her physical frenzy began to calm.

"Me too." He kissed her back.

Monika closed her eyes. James held her firmly.

They both fell into a peaceful sleep. The sheer curtain had stopped billowing and the moonlight was now brightly cast upon them.

●

Monika was first to awaken. The sunlight was shining through the window of her second story bedroom. James was still asleep. She decided not to disturb him. She checked the time on her bedside clock: 8:00 AM. There was still plenty of time. Their flight did not leave 'til noon.

She lay there and watched as James slept. Ever since the episode in San Francisco they had been together. It seemed like yesterday that they had met, but it was two years ago. Since that time they had lived together. Monika wondered if they would ever marry. She wanted to start a family— to have James' children. She wondered when James would ask her.

They had both been so busy after San Francisco. James had been assigned to several long cases which had taken him away from her for several weeks at a time, and Monika had written her first bestselling novel, OBSESSION, which had been based upon her parents' disappearance and the San Francisco FBI chief agent, Mical Grai, who was behind it. The book had been published three months ago and Monika found herself busy with promotions and appearances that had been arranged by her publisher. There was even negotiations going on for film rights. As a result, she and James had not had much personal time together.

Monika hoped that this trip would change

things. She had been invited to The Festival of Writers in Toronto—or Emerald City as she now called it because of a building that was apparently made out of gold—an image that was to her, very unreal, belonging to the 'land of Oz', to read from OBSESSION. Monika had learnt about this building in the information pamphlet that the festival had forwarded to her. She was amused by the decadence of such a structure and the irony, during these hard times, of the fact that it was the head office of a bank. The festival was only a weekend trip, but she and James had decided to extend their stay and make a week of it. It would be a nice vacation—the first vacation that they had taken together.

James and Monika had never been to Toronto, but they had heard many good things about this Canadian business center. Monika's reading was a great opportunity for them to get away and visit this foreign northern place. They were looking forward to visiting Monika's 'Emerald City'. Monika especially hoped that this trip would strengthen her relationship with James and perhaps help them become even closer. 'Perhaps he might pop the question?' Monika mused, then mentally shook herself. It was time to get ready. There would be plenty of time for these thoughts in 'Emerald City'.

Monika gently placed her hand upon James' chest and began to rouse him.

"James. James," she said lovingly. "It's time sweetie. We've got to get up. James," she repeated.

James gradually awoke. He opened his eyes and smiled as he saw Monika's beautiful smile and blue eyes.

"Good morning." He smiled and put his arms around her. He stretched and yawned as he became more awake.

"We've got to get going or we'll miss the flight."

James rolled over with Monika in his arms, pinning her underneath him.

"We could always catch the next flight." There was a mischievous glint in his eyes. Monika understood his meaning.

"No. Not now!" Monika was flattered and playful. "Wasn't last night enough?"

"Enough?" James feigned shock. "It's never enough."

They playfully wrestled with each other. Monika was trying to squirm away while James tried to convince her to partake in more passion. There was laughter. Just as Monika was about to give in, the phone rang. James focused on Monika and ignored the ringing.

"Stop," Monika pleaded in a playful tone. "It might be about the flight."

James continued to ignore the phone.

"Stop." Monika became firm. James rolled off

her, lay back on the pillow and smiled.

"Okay. Two minutes, but if it's your mother…" he shook his finger at Monika, playfully scolding her.

"Oh. Yeah. In your dreams." Monika shook her head in response as she stretched over to answer the phone. James made one last attempt and kissed her exposed soft buttock.

"Stop it." Monika was not really complaining.

James stopped and pretended to sulk.

"That's it. You're cut off," Monika teased, as she reached the phone.

"Hello," she answered. "Yes. Just a minute please." Monika put her hand over the mouth piece. "It's for you." She smirked.

"Who?" James whispered.

"I don't know. Don't be long. I'll go and shower." Monika took advantage of the opportunity and slid out of bed as she handed the phone to James.

"Hello?" James immediately sobered up.

He watched Monika as she walked across the room. She was beautiful in her petite nakedness. She was putting up her strawberry blonde hair and sensed him watching. She turned to check. Her beautiful blue eyes sparkled with life. He smiled and blew her a kiss. She feigned shyness and hurried to the bathroom to shower and get ready. She was very happy. It was going to be such a lovely trip. She believed that things were about to change for the better.

"Yes. Yes." James was not saying much on the phone. "But sir. I…" he tried to speak but was cut off. His mood had changed and he was now sitting on the edge of the bed. His body was tense.

"But I'm going away today." As he spoke he leaned over to his pants that were draped over a chair and pulled out a tiny blue felt pouch. He opened it and gently shook until a beautiful ring appeared. He had planned to give it to Monika on their trip and ask her to marry him.

The ring was yellow eighteen carat gold with a large cluster of diamonds surrounded by small rubies. It had cost him two months' salary, but it was worth it.

There was more conversation, followed by a series of acknowledgments. James slid the ring back into its protective pouch and returned it to his pants pocket. It would have to wait. He was disappointed, but it was beyond his control. He would now have to find another suitable time and place to ask her.

"Yes. Yes. I understand." There was obviously no choice in the matter. James' tone was no longer arguing, but accepting. "I'll be there in an hour." He hung up the phone and sat silently considering how he was going to tell Monika.

A few moments after James hung up the phone Monika came back into the room. She had showered and was dressed in her white lace bra and panties. A towel was wrapped around her wet hair.

"So what do you think?" she asked as she modeled the new undergarments for James.

"Nice." James' tone was distant. Monika picked it up right away.

"Who was that on the phone?" She stopped modeling and prepared herself for some bad news. There were several awkward moments. James stood up from the bed.

"They need me at the office," he said. He did not look Monika in the eyes as he spoke. "Sorry. I can't go."

James walked past her and down the hall to the bathroom to get ready. Monika followed after him in unbelieving shock.

"What do you mean?! Sorry?"

James made no response, but kept walking down the hall and into the bathroom.

Monika stopped half way down the hall and watched him in disappointment and frustration. She stood there waiting for his reply.

"What am I supposed to do? I have to go." she continued trying to elicit a response from him.

James slammed the bathroom door shut and ended the confrontation.

"Oo wha!" Monika was disappointed and livid. She shook her head, turned and went back into her room. This was so unfair. This was so much like her last relationship, with William. She admonished herself for being so stupid to allow herself to fall into a similar relationship.

She felt like crying, but fought the urge. No, she would not cry. She would not be weak. She sat on her bed and composed herself. She could hear the shower running. Determinedly, she got up from the bed and crossed to her closet. She took out the dress that she had chosen the night before. As she began to dress she spoke firmly to herself.

"Well. If that's the way you want it. Fine. I'll go myself. Who needs this anyway."

Monika quickly dressed, removed the towel and combed her hair. She walked out of the room and down the hall. Stopping at the bathroom door she could still hear the sound of James showering. She hesitated a moment and then, finalizing her decision, continued past the bathroom and down the stairs to the front entrance.

There were two bags next to the door. She picked up one, and then took some keys from the brass tray on the small entry table. Putting her hand upon the door handle she stopped to consider one last time. The shower was still on. She was very disappointed. She opened the door and left the house.

She walked down the front pathway to the red Corvette in the driveway. Unlocking the driver's door she threw her bag into the passenger's seat and then got into the vehicle. She was angry as she put the key into the ignition and started the car. She put the car into reverse and squealed out of the driveway into the street. She forced the car into drive. She squealed the tires again and drove off.

Not long after Monika's departure, James had finished his shower. He had wrapped a towel around his waist and exited the bathroom. He felt bad about disappointing Monika, but there was nothing he could do. He called out her name from the hallway.

"Monika?" There was no response. The house was very quiet. "Monika?"

James assumed that Monika was sulking and would not answer. He shook his head in disapproval of what he considered her childish behavior.

"Monika?" he called out again as he made his way down the hall and to the bedroom where he expected to find her.

"I'm sorry, but I didn't have a choice. It's some sort of emergency and they're calling in my whole section…" As he spoke these last words he entered into the bedroom.

He was surprised not to find Monika there. His attitude changed. He examined the room and noted that the closet door was open. An empty hanger stood out. James noted that Monika's watch was also gone from her dressing table.

"Monika?" he again called out. This time there was a note of panic in his voice.

James turned and went down the hall.

"Monika!" he called out to the house below from the upper landing. Still there was no answer.

The realization of what might have occurred struck home. James hurried down the stairs to the front door.

"Monika?" He saw the missing luggage and car keys.

He opened the door and ran out into the front yard. The car was gone. He was angered by Monika's desertion, and stomped his foot then shook his head. As he did this the towel around his waist came loose and fell to the ground. He quickly bent to pick it up and cover himself. He became more angered by this embarrassment and the realization that he now had no transportation to get to the office.

●

When Monika arrived at LAX she pulled up in front of the departure level for American Airlines and stopped the car at the curb in a tow away zone. She wanted to punish James for his inability to say no to his boss and go on the trip. She had had a long cry during her journey to the airport and was trying to remain strong and determined to follow through and go to Emerald City. After all, the reading had been arranged long ago and she was certain there had been advertising materials sent out to the local area. She couldn't cancel at this late time.

Whether James came with her or not she had to go—she wanted to go, but she also had wanted him to come with her. She understood that his job was important, but she was not sure she wanted to be in another relationship like the one she had had with William. She wanted more of a commitment to her and the relationship.

She took the key out of the ignition and opened the car door. As she got out, she called a Red Cap to help her with her luggage. The Red Cap hurried over to her.

"Morning Ma'am." He did not comment on where Monika had parked.

"I'm on American flight 291 to Toronto. Can you take that bag?" She indicated her large bag on the passenger's seat.

"Certainly, Ma'am." The Red Cap tried the door. It was locked.

"Oh. It's locked. Just a minute." Monika leaned back into the car and unlocked the doors by pushing the power unlock button. The passenger door lock immediately shot open.

The Red Cap opened the door and pulled out the luggage which he put on a little trolley that was beside him.

"Anything else, Ma'am?" he asked as he closed the door.

"No. That's it. Thank you." Monika closed her door and walked up to the entrance to the airport terminal, taking the keys with her and leaving the car unattended. The Red Cap followed her.

When they arrived at the check-in counter, Monika thanked the Red Cap and gave him a five dollar tip.

The Red Cap was pleased. "What about your car Ma'am? You can't leave it there. It will get towed." He was polite.

"Don't worry about it. It's not my car. It's my boyfriend's problem now." Monika's tone was clear.

The Red Cap understood. As he walked away he chuckled at the situation and the obvious fact that this woman was mad at her boyfriend. He muttered to himself some comment about fury and a woman scorned.

Monika was early. There was no waiting as she went up to the ticket agent to check in. As she handed the agent her ticket, she looked around, silently hoping that James would change his mind and join her on the flight. Though she knew this was not likely, she hoped it would happen. She hoped that James would drop everything to be with her. She hoped that she had not made a mistake.

"That's seat 10A. Boarding through gate 8. You can go ahead now if you like and wait at the gate. I'll check your bag through," The agent said interrupting Monika's thoughts.

"Oh. Yes. Thank you." Monika took the documents from the agent. She was not paying complete attention. Her thoughts were still on James. She was very upset at the reality of her present situation. She decided to wait for a short while at the gate. Perhaps James would still show up.

Chapter 2

"Excuse me Miss," the flight attendant directed her words to Monika. "Miss?"

Monika had fallen asleep after she had finished the in-flight meal. She did not wish to watch the movie. She wanted to sleep. It had been a busy day and she was still upset about James letting her down. She had put on her headset but did not turn on any program, in order not to be disturbed by anyone. She wanted to be left alone to her own thoughts. She sat and became mesmerized by the muted sounds of the plane as it flew. The constant roar of the engines reminded her of the sound of waves on a rough day at the ocean as they crashed upon the beach. She closed her eyes and was caressed by the sound. It did not take long for her to fall into sleep.

Time passed without her conscious notice. Three hours later the plane was reaching its destination. The flight attendant who had left Monika undisturbed for the whole trip now leaned over from the aisle and gently touched Monika's left arm. She spoke gently over the noise of the now whining engines. The plane had started its descent; in about fifteen minutes they would arrive.

"Miss? Miss?" She tried once and then again.

Monika opened her eyes. "Yes?"

"We're getting ready to land. You'll have to put your seat up and fasten your belt." The flight attendant smiled and then moved on down the aisle.

Monika nodded her acknowledgement. She removed the headset and, finding the button on the right arm rest, raised her seat back to its original upright position. She noted that the 'no smoking—fasten seat belts' sign was illuminated. Still a little groggy, she slid the window blind up and gazed out the window. It was late in the day here. The sun was setting. She looked at her wristwatch: 5:10 PM California time. That meant it was... she thought a moment, 8:10 PM here. There was a three hour time difference. After fastening her seat belt, she sat back in her chair and watched through the window. There was no one seated next to her.

Monika was intrigued by the sights as they passed. Below there was an incredible mass of water that looked like it might be an ocean. The setting sun was glistening and reflecting upon it. Ahead in the distance was the coastline of Lake Ontario. She remembered studying about Lake Ontario in high school, but had never realized its vastness. Even from this height, she could not see the other shores that surrounded it. It was more like the ocean approach to San Francisco than a lake.

Gradually the plane descended and approached the land mass ahead. The plane was still over the blue water of the lake. The land ahead was brown and green in color. Somehow Monika had expected there to be ice and snow. She knew that it was summer here, but she had always thought of Canada as the land of winter.

Within minutes the plane crossed over the shoreline and left the lake behind. Below was a great mass of what she thought was farmland. The land was divided up into a series of rectangular shapes and earth tone colors. Neat farms and fields presented a patchwork quilt of greens, browns and greys. It was a predominately flat landscape with a slight roll to it. There were roads and a few buildings that were quite scattered. It was hard to make out exactly what the structures actually were from so high up.

The plane followed the shoreline as it continued to descend. Gradually the scenery changed from less populated and isolated rural to the beginnings of what Monika believed must be the surrounding suburban area of Emerald City.

As the plane banked and turned, Monika caught a glimpse of the skyline of the city. It was not far away. She marveled at how suddenly out of nothing the city had appeared. It was a beautiful sight. Centrally clustered near the lake were the skyscrapers of the downtown area. There were many high buildings but highest amongst them all was a tower that pierced high into the clouds.

The city faced south and was situated on land that jutted into the lake. There was a golden glow which seemed to emanate from the buildings of the downtown area, but was really being reflected upon them from the lake and the setting sun. The plane banked again, hiding the city from view.

For the first time Monika felt good about her decision to come here alone. She had been worried that she might be going to a place that was in the middle of nowhere. In reality, Emerald City appeared to be a large thriving city, one that, on a smaller scale, reminded her of New York or San Francisco. She felt as if she was at home. It was hard to explain, but she thought it must be due to the modern skyscrapers and their proximity to the water.

The plane was going lower and lower in its

approach. Monika was soon able to easily make out the highways below and could clearly see the cars driving on them. The roads were not very busy. Everything seemed so clean and fresh. This pleased Monika. 'All the benefits of a city without the massive sprawl or mess,' she thought to herself.

Suddenly there was a loud mechanical whining and a thud as the landing gear was lowered and locked into place. It would not be long now. The plane was in its final approach to the airport. Below, the area was very industrial, but clean. There was a large multi-lane highway.

The plane flew lower and lower 'til it seemed that it was going to land on the highway. Then out of nowhere appeared the runway to the airport. The plane crossed over the highway and dropped quickly onto the runway. There was the bounce of the plane's wheels touching down. Once, twice, then on the third touch the plane had landed. A cheer and applause broke out from the other passengers on the plane. Monika thought it odd that people would react in such a way. Landing safely was surely the least the pilot should do.

The pilot, as if reacting to his audience, spoke over the intercom. "Welcome to Toronto. The temperature is a cool twelve degrees Celsius and the forecast for the next few days is clear and warm. On behalf of the crew and myself, thank you for flying American today. We hope your stay is a pleasant one."

Los Angeles was far behind her. Monika turned her attention to getting ready to deplane.

The plane taxied along and slowly pulled into the terminal; a terminal that looked very similar to the airports she was used to in the United States. Somehow she had expected there to be many differences here in this foreign country, but everything seemed similar, only on a smaller scale. It was as if she had never left home.

Once the plane had stopped at the gate, Monika got up and made her way amongst the other passengers down the aisle toward the front exit of the plane. Flight attendants stood at the exit saying good-bye. Monika smiled and acknowledged them as she passed by and then stepped out of the plane onto the gangway.

The journey from the plane into the main terminal was a long one. The corridors Monika followed had no windows to the outside. It felt claustrophobic. Monika walked along, following the passengers ahead of her, and soon came to an escalator which took her down to a large room. This was Canadian Immigration. Monika took her place in a small line and waited her turn to go through immigration. As she waited, she noted the signs that informed people of where they were and what they had to do. Everything was written twice: once in English and once in French. She felt happy to be here. It felt quaint. It would be nice to do her reading and then explore this city.

"Next."

Monika's turn arrived. She crossed the red wait-ing line marked on the carpet and walked to the counter of the immigration agent. She handed the agent her documents. Monika found his uniform very formal and British in appearance.

"Purpose of your stay?" the agent inquired.

"Vacation." Monika replied. It was always best to keep it simple with immigration agents.

"How long will you stay?"

"One week."

"Will you be visiting a farm?"

"No." Monika thought this a strange question.

"Thank you." The agent returned her documents and gave her a slip of paper. "Give this to customs after you get your bags."

Monika smiled, took back the documents and moved on. She followed the other cleared passen-gers down another corridor and soon arrived at the large baggage claim area.

There was a large conveyor belt coming out of one part of the wall of the area. Its path ran and weaved its way like a serpent along the length of the room before it disappeared back into another opening in the wall at the far end of the room. The belt was not yet activated. Passengers were stand-ing along it waiting for their luggage to appear. Monika took up a position close to the beginning of the belt. She wanted to get going. She was being met by a car and taken to a hotel in the city. It had all been prearranged through the festival and her publisher. The plane had arrived on schedule. She wanted to quickly get to the hotel and relax.

The schedule for her participation in the festival started tomorrow, Sunday. Her reading was at 2:00 PM. The Canadian representatives of her publisher would meet her for lunch tomorrow and escort her to the event. Tonight, after she checked into the hotel, was her own.

The conveyor belt sprang to life. After a few moments baggage started to appear on it. Everyone was watching and waiting to identify their own belongings. As they did, they quickly grabbed hold of them, pulling them quickly from the conveyor belt.

Monika saw her bag. It was slowly moving her way. When it arrived she picked it up and placed it on the floor. It had tiny wheels of its own. She started for the exit, rolling it behind her, to the final customs agent that awaited there.

Monika came up to the customs agent and handed in the slip of paper that the immigration officer had given her. The customs agent took the paper and, after taking a very quick glance at it, passed her on.

"Have a nice stay," the agent said.

"Thank you." How polite everyone seemed, Monika silently observed.

Once past customs Monika went through a large automated sliding opaque door and into the arrivals area of the terminal. There was a crowd of people and limousine drivers lined up. The drivers were holding small handwritten signs with names of their pick-ups.

Monika began to look for a sign with her name. She made her way through the crowd and there, next to the main terminal exit, was a man dressed in a chauffeur's uniform holding a sign in front of him: 'QUELLER'. Monika walked up to him.

"Hi. I'm Monika Queller."

"Good evening, Miss Queller." The man put away his sign. "May I take your bag?" The man was polite. He spoke with an accent, but Monika could not make it out.

"Yes. Thank you." Monika allowed the chauffeur to take her bag.

"I'm parked just outside. Please…"

The chauffeur indicated that she should go ahead through the exit and that he would follow.

Outside, there was a large black limousine waiting in front of the doors. Monika was impressed. She felt like a celebrity. Many eyes were turned her way as the chauffeur opened her door and helped her into the back of the limousine. He closed the door and proceeded to the back of the car and opened the trunk. He placed Monika's bag in the trunk, closed it and continued on to his driver's side. All his motions were smooth and efficient. He was obviously concerned not to keep his charge waiting any longer than necessary.

Inside, the limousine was very plush and comfortable. Monika sat in the middle of the soft dark leather seat. There was a remarkable amount of room inside. The area could easily seat six people in comfort. The carpeting was thick and a clean light grey in color. The windows were all darkly tinted. Monika could see out, but no one, she imagined, would be able look in. In front of her was a small table made out of a dark mahogany. It was very shiny and upon it was a small glass and a small bottle of expensive champagne that was open and chilling in a clear container of ice. Monika leaned forward, picked up the bottle out of its carafe, and poured half a glass of the champagne. She sat back and sipped on the champagne and watched the busy outside world from which she now felt protected in this cocoon.

The driver got into the car. His section was separated from Monika's compartment by a dark glass partition. Without saying a word to his passenger or even looking in her direction, he drove out into the main flow of traffic. Monika did not question the driver, but sank deeper back into the cozy seat and enjoyed the sights.

The limousine made its way through the maze of airport roadways and finally to a major highway. Monika could not see very much, but it was clear to her that this was a major metropolitan area. Outside it was beginning to get dark. She checked her watch: 8:55 PM. The lights of the highway were just coming on and glittered through the approaching dusk.

After ten minutes or so the lights of the downtown core came into view. It was a magnificent sight to behold. The CN Tower was in the center of the skyline, flashing with several warning lights. The car was going in the direction of the downtown corridor and the lake front. As the limousine was now much closer to them, the size of the CN Tower and the other downtown buildings appeared larger. Monika knew she was staying at the waterfront in the Weston Hotel, but she had not realized how centrally located the hotel was.

As they progressed, the highway began to run parallel to the lakeshore and directly toward the Tower. After another ten minutes the roadway began to rise up above ground level about four stories. It was obviously some sort of expressway into the city. To the right could be seen the harbor area and a set of islands about half a mile offshore from the downtown core. There were many boats out in this naturally protected area sailing to and fro.

The expressway soon found its way into the city. The lights of the buildings on the left and the sparkle of the activity on the lake to the right in the harbor were spectacular from the raised vista of the expressway. The Tower soon rose up next to the roadway. The limousine approached and passed under it. Monika strained to look up its height.

Immediately after passing the Tower, the driver started to pull off from the expressway and prepared to exit into what Monika believed was the middle of the highest buildings of the city at the waterfront. The whole area was unbelievably beautiful and clean!

There was so much to see that Monika had not noticed the sign of the hotel as the limousine turned and drove up the steep driveway of the Weston Hotel. The driveway was all enclosed. Many little lights lit the driveway from the ceiling above. It reminded her of a Hollywood premiere.

The limousine drove up to the main entrance and stopped. Monika sat in anticipation. There was a large glass entry running the whole length of the limousine and more. Two glass revolving doors were in the center and several doormen and porters, dressed in dark green jackets, were standing about or helping any new arrivals. As the car stopped in front of the revolving doors, one of the doormen came up to Monika's limousine and opened her door.

"Good evening. Are you a guest of the hotel?" The man spoke softly in what Monika identified as a British accent.

"Yes. Thank you." Monika slid over to the open door and began to get out of the car. The doorman helped her out.

"Thank you." Monika repeated as she was helped out.

"The front desk is inside to your left. I'll see to your luggage," the doorman directed Monika and then walked to the back of the car where the chauffeur was already waiting. Monika went through one of the revolving doors and into the lobby of the hotel.

The lobby was very large with a modern open concept design. It looked like it had been recently built. To the right was a twenty-foot wide hallway with two shops on either side and an entry to a small lounge. To the left was a roped area where the concierge had his table. A little farther along was a set of narrow escalators going up and down. Directly south of the escalators was the mahogany countertop of the front desk, which ran about twenty-five feet. There were several people being serviced by four or five employees. The men were neatly attired in dark green blazers, black pants, white shirts and ties, while the women wore green blazers, white blouses and black skirts.

Directly in front of the revolving doors about twenty feet away was a step-down, open concept, lobby lounge. There were many people sitting around relaxing and chatting. A waitress was taking orders.

Ceiling to floor windows lined the lobby

lounge's southern wall exposure which over-looked what appeared to be a park, and then a hundred or so feet away the protected harbor of the lake. The sound of a pianist softly playing a baby grand piano off in the left corner of the lounge could be heard. Separating the lobby lounge from the main entrance to the hotel was a half wall of planters full of small shrubs, flowers and bonsai trees. In front of the planters, and before the opening of the main entrance, were a series of seating areas stretching in front of the lobby lounge. Each seating area was composed of small circular tables surrounded by light blue two-person leather sofas. There was a very relaxed feel to the place.

Pleased with what she had seen so far, Monika made her way over to the front desk to check in.

"Hi. I have a reservation," Monika said to the woman desk clerk as she came to the counter.

"What name is the reservation under?"

"Queller. Monika Queller."

The woman typed in the name on the keyboard in front of her and then watched her monitor. Instantly Monika's reservation was confirmed.

"Yes, Ms. Queller. I have it here." There was a pause. "The weekend is taken care of. How long will you be staying?"

"'Til next Saturday."

"Oh yes. Here it is. The extra days are con-firmed. Did you want it on the credit card you made the reservation with?"

"Yes."

The woman did some more typing and then a small printer beside the monitor began to type out a form. She tore it from the machine and placed it on the countertop between them.

"If you could sign here and please put down your home address? Will you be needing parking? One or two room keys?'

"No." Monika was writing her address on the card. The question about two keys made her momentarily think of James. She was still angry that he had not come with her.

"Just one will be fine." She continued writing. When she had finished she handed it back to the woman.

"Thank you." The woman took the form and in turn gave Monika a tiny credit card key.

"Put the key arrow down to unlock your room door." She indicated a large arrow printed on one side of the card. "Room 1711 South. I've given you a corner suite facing the city and lake." She smiled.

"Thank you." Monika turned to walk away.

"Ms. Queller." The woman stopped her. "There are some messages for you."

The woman went to a row of tiny boxes and took out a couple of envelopes from the one marked 1711 S and came back to the counter. She handed them to Monika.

"Do you need help with your bags?"

"Thank you. Yes," Monika answered as she curiously took and looked through the envelopes. She wondered who would have left messages for her.

The desk clerk rang for the Bell Captain. A smartly dressed young man appeared.

"Take Ms. Queller's bags to 1711 South," she directed.

The young man looked to Monika,

"Follow me, Ma'am." He already had her bag in his hand. He had been at the entrance when Monika arrived and taken it from the chauffeur after Monika had gone into the hotel. Monika had not even been aware of him.

"Thank you." Monika was impressed. "Thank you," she said to the desk clerk.

"You're welcome. Have a pleasant stay."

The young porter led the way and crossed through the lobby to a set of four elevators. There was one elevator waiting. He pleasantly directed Monika into the elevator and followed after her. Monika enjoyed his chivalrous behavior even if it was his job to be helpful.

Once in, the porter pushed 17. The doors slid shut and the elevator started to rise. After a couple of floors the elevator was suddenly exposed to the outside. Monika turned to look through the back window of the elevator and behold the magnificent view of the city lights as the elevator climbed higher. It truly was a spectacular place. Upon arriving at their floor, the porter got out and led Monika down the hall to her room.

"May I have your key, Ma'am?" he asked when they came to 1711.

"Yes." Monika gave him the key and watched as he placed it in the lock mechanism. A green light went on and the door unlocked. The porter pulled out the key, pushed down the door handle and opened the door.

"After you, Ma'am."

"Thank you."

The room was very large. As Monika entered, she came into a large sitting room that was comfortably decorated with antique style furniture. She went over to the large picture window but it was hard to see much as it was now dark outside. The window overlooked the harbor and the lake.

The porter walked through the sitting room and opened two large doors.

"Shall I put your bag in your room?"

"Yes, thank you." She would check out the bedroom after the porter left.

The porter entered the bedroom and quickly returned.

"Will there be anything else?" he asked.

"No. Thank you." Monika handed him a large tip. The porter saw it and was pleased.

"Thank you." He put the room key on the table in the middle of the sitting room and left.

"Wow. This is incredible," Monika said out loud to herself. She crossed the sitting room and went into the bedroom.

The bedroom was as large as the sitting room. It was also nicely decorated in antique style furnishings—very European looking. The queen-size bed was placed against a wall opposite another large picture window to take advantage of the spectacular view. This window overlooked the city and was ablaze with its sparkling lights. Placed on the bed was a wicker basket, wrapped in clear plastic, containing a selection of fruits, chocolates and biscuits. Monika went over to it. There was a card taped to the wrapping. She picked up the card, and read 'Welcome to the Festival of Writers.' It was signed Craig Gatten.

How nice. He was the organizer of the festival. This basket was a very romantic and thoughtful touch—she did not want to ruin it. She would open it later. It had been a long day and she wanted to indulge in a hot soak and have an early night. Tomorrow was going to be a hectic day.

She placed her handbag and the envelopes from the front desk on the bedside table and moved the basket onto a chair behind her. She plopped herself down on the bed. It was very soft. She rested a moment and then decided to see who had left her messages. Monika stretched over and took the two envelopes from the table.

Both envelopes were plain and had her name

typed on them. The first was a note from her Canadian publisher welcoming her and was personally signed by Bob Bron. He said he would meet her mid-morning for coffee in the lobby lounge and that he would call before he came.

Monika was being treated royally. She was happy her book had obviously caught the attention of the reading public even here in Emerald City. It was amazing how she had become a novelist.

Monika had written OBSESSION very soon after her experience in San Francisco. She had written several short fantasy stories in the past, but they had never been published. She thought they were better stories, but it was her mystery novel based on her true life experience that had become a bestseller. Now she went on trips and was becoming successful as a writer. It was OBSESSION that had brought her here to Emerald City.

She put down Bob's letter and opened the second envelope. It contained the itinerary of her day at the festival. She put both letters back on the bedside table. She would look at them again later. Right now she wanted to get out of her traveling clothes and into a hot bath.

Monika went into the bathroom, which was also in an antique motif and very bright. There were all the usual facilities and also a very big whirlpool bath. The room was huge. She took several steps to the bathtub and, leaning over, depressed the drain plug and ran the water, checking its temperature as it came from the spout.

On the side of the tub was a package of bubble bath. Monika opened the package to smell its aroma. It was soft and sweet. She poured it into the bath under the flow of the water and turned to leave the room. On the bathroom door there was a thick white cotton bathrobe. She took the robe off its hook and left.

Going back into the bedroom, she removed her dress and undergarments and put on the white hotel bathrobe. Just as she was putting on the robe there was a loud knock at the door. She wondered who it was. She tightened the drawstring, securing the robe firmly, and went to see who it was.

Monika was a little concerned to receive a knock this late in the evening in a strange city. She would be careful not to open the door until she knew who it was. As she neared the room door she saw a white envelope under the door that had been slid through from the other side. She cautiously came over and picked up the envelope. There was nothing written upon it. She then carefully checked the hall through the peep hole of the door, but no one was there in front of her door. It was very odd. Monika felt a little afraid. Leaning against the door, she broke the seal of the envelope to see what was inside. She looked in and discovered a clipping from a newspaper. She removed it and started to read the article.

'MAN FOUND SHOT AT AIRPORT LOUNGE' was the headline. The article was from the Toronto Daily News and was dated about two weeks ago. The article told the gruesome story of a man, Ted Ambrose, who had been shot once in the head and had had his left hand chopped off. Apparently there were no leads and the police were requesting help from anyone who might have been at the airport or seen this man on the day of the shooting.

There was nothing else in the envelope. Monika wondered why it had been slid under her door. She wondered if it had been a mistake and meant for someone else. She placed the article back into the envelope and decided to give it no more thought. She was tired and wanted to slip into her hot bath.

Chapter 3

The ring of the phone wakened Monika from a sound sleep. Groggily she picked up the receiver.

"Hello?"

"It's your nine o'clock wake up call Ms. Queller," came the voice of the hotel operator.

"Thank you." Monika hung up the phone. She had requested the wake up call last night after her bath and before she had jumped into her cozy bed. She wanted to be awake before the room service she ordered for 9:15 AM arrived.

The room was very bright. She could see that the sky was clear blue and the sun strong. She had not drawn the curtains before going to bed. There was no need. There were no other tall buildings nearby. No one would be peeping in on her.

Monika lay there a moment to more fully awaken. Eventually, she threw back the covers and got up from bed. She was wearing a pair of James' white silk pajamas. She liked to wear them. They felt good against her skin even if the thin fabric revealed more than it concealed.

Getting out of bed, she put on the hotel bathrobe and her wristwatch which was lying on the bedside table. She checked her appearance in the mirror that was mounted on the open closet door of the bedroom. After fluffing her hair into place, she walked from the bedroom and into the large sitting room. She stood looking out of the window over the harbor, islands and lake.

The harbor was full of life. There were hundreds of small sailing dinghies, larger sail boats and a couple of Mississippi Riverboat style ferries going to and from the island and the city. Off to the southwest there was a small airport with light planes taking off and approaching to land. The lake was a dark blue-green and reflected the early morning rising sun.

Monika was interrupted by a rapid knocking at the door and someone calling out "Room service."

This was her breakfast. Monika checked the time on her wristwatch—9:15 AM. Right on time. She crossed over to and opened the door.

"Good morning. Here is your breakfast. It's

going to be lovely day. I hope you had pleasant sleep." The maid kept up a cheerful constant chatter as she rolled a trolley into the room and proceeded to place all the plates of food on the table in the center of the sitting room. She was Filipina and spoke with a tiny high pitched voice in broken English.

Monika did not say much. She was amused by the maid's performance. Before she knew it, the maid was finished.

"Will there be anything else, Ma'am?" The maid offered a pen and a bill for Monika to sign.

"No. Thank you." Monika added a large tip and signed the chit.

"Thank you very much, Ma'am." The maid became even more cordial as she noted the tip and made a little curtsy before taking the trolley and leaving. Monika sat down and began to eat her meal.

As she was eating, the phone rang. Monika stretched over and picked up the receiver to the phone on a nearby table.

"Hello?"

"Ms. Queller?"

"Yes?"

"Bob Bron of Simon Books Canada."

"Oh yes. Hello Mr. Bron."

"Please…Bob. Did you have a good trip? Is the room okay?"

"Yes. Everything is lovely. Thank you."

"It's the least we can do for our newest best-selling author." Bob spoke with a warm, welcoming tone.

"Well, thank you anyway. It is very nice and the room is much more than I expected."

"Did you get my note?"

"Yes."

"Good. Will 11:00 AM in the lobby lounge be okay?"

"Yes that will be fine."

"Good, that will give us a chance to get to know one another and allow me go over the schedule for the day."

"That will be fine. By the way, Bob," Monika, remembering the other envelope asked, "did you put another envelope under my door last night?"

"No. I left two at the front desk. Why?"

"Oh nothing. Just something that someone must have mistakenly left. It's not important."

"I'll see you at eleven then."

"Okay."

Monika took the receiver from her ear and placed it back in its cradle. She again wondered who had sent her the news clipping, but it was impossible to guess. There was no point in dwelling on it. She shrugged it off. There was no time to waste on such things. She wanted to finish her breakfast, shower and get dressed. It was going to be an exciting day.

●

At 10:55 Monika got off the elevator on the main level of the hotel. There were a lot of people milling about. The brightness of the day shone through the large lobby lounge windows, bathing the whole area in a soft, summery light. She was dressed in a smart, what she termed, power suit. It was dark and she had a gold brooch which elegantly stood out on her left lapel. A tiny Chanel purse hung from her shoulder. Many eyes were upon her as she crossed the distance to the entrance of the lobby lounge. Just in front of the lounge, there was a slender man in his early forties dressed in a midnight blue double-breasted suit. He had a mustache and appeared quite debonair.

"Monika." The man offered his hand as she approached. "Bob Bron. Nice to finally meet you. You're even lovelier than your book jacket picture."

Monika was flattered. "Hello. Thank you." She shook his hand.

"Shall we have a coffee and go over the plans for the day?"

"Sure."

Bob led Monika into the lounge to a small circular table with two vacant high-back covered chairs in front of the window overlooking the lake and the ferry docks. As they sat, Monika noticed the crowds of people lining up to get on the ferry.

"Two coffees." Bob caught the waitress as she

was walking by and then sat down. He noticed that Monika was observing the sights. "How do you like our city so far?"

"It's lovely. I didn't expect it to be so…" she searched for the correct words, not wanting to insult Bob.

"Sophisticated?"

"Yes. No offense but I didn't realize that it was such a big city."

"Yes. We have grown a lot over the past few years." Bob changed the subject. "Did you know that your book is a bestseller in Canada?"

"No." Monika felt pleased.

"It's a nice story. You write well."

"Thank you."

"I would imagine that there will be quite a large crowd at the festival waiting to meet you."

"What time is the reading?" Monika changed the direction of the conversation. Though she was pleased that the book was selling well, she felt uncomfortable with all the attention that a successful book was starting to bring.

"They've moved it up to one this afternoon. Is that alright?"

"Oh that's fine."

"After the reading there will be a little reception in your honor. Some local press will be there. After that we're done."

"It sounds good."

"I understand you are staying on for the week?"

"Yes. I thought it would be a nice time of year to have a vacation and explore the city."

"Yes. Except for yesterday, it has been a very warm summer so far. Would you mind coming to our office at some point and meeting some of the sales reps?"

"Certainly. I wouldn't mind at all."

"Good, I'll arrange it with you later."

The coffee arrived. The waitress placed two tea-spoons, cups and saucers, a carafe of coffee, cream and sugar upon the small table. Both Monika and Bob thanked her as she left, and then continued their conversation about the day's events and expectations.

On the other side of the room, Bob and Monika were being watched by a good-looking, svelte young man in his twenties. He was dressed in casual clothing. He was nervously sipping from a cup and pretending to be reading a newspaper, being careful not to be noticed by them. In all the excitement of the moment, neither Monika nor Bob did.

Chapter 4

Monika and Bob arrived at the festival auditorium at 12:40 PM. They had taken a cab from the hotel. It was a short distance down the street from the hotel to the harborfront building that housed the festival. Being such a lovely warm summer day, the harbor area was quite busy with people. Amongst them was the young man who had been watching Monika and Bob in the lobby lounge. He had left the lounge right after them. He knew where they were going. He had a ticket for Monika's reading.

The cab ride took only five minutes. They could have walked, but Bob thought it better to ride.

"Here we are," Bob announced. He leaned over and paid the driver, then opened the door and got out first. Monika got out on her side and walked around the cab to the entrance of the building they had pulled up in front of.

The building was an old converted warehouse. There was a sign above the main entrance— 'Harborside'. It was situated adjacent to the harbor opposite another warehouse that had been refurbished into shops and condominiums. Oddly, it reminded Monika of Ghirardelli Square in San Francisco and, by association, the experience that had occurred there. She decided to read from that section of her book.

They walked into the building and were greeted by a rotund little man dressed in a very conservative suit and tie.

"Bob. Welcome. This must be Ms. Queller. Right on time. Hi, I'm Craig Gatten." He spoke in a pretentious, affected manner. Monika was not sure how to react. He seemed an odd character.

"Hi. Nice to meet you." Monika took his hand. It was a very limp shake.

"You've got quite a crowd for your reading. Let's go inside. The show must go on." Gatten almost pirouetted as he turned to lead them down the hall to the stage entrance of the auditorium. "If you wait here, I'll go in and introduce you. Sorry for the rush, but it's just about time."

"Thanks Craig," Bob spoke on Monika's behalf.

Gatten went inside. Monika could hear the crowd within as she stood next to the open doorway. In a few moments Gatten was in front of the audience beginning Monika's introduction. Monika watched from the doorway.

"He's a little odd?" she commented to Bob.

"Yes. He's got a bit of an ego and everyone knows he's a jerk, but he's got connections and somehow manages to keep this job."

"Oh. Nepotism."

"Yep. Just humor him. Do you have a book to read from?"

"Yes. It's in my purse." Monika opened her purse and took out a black paperback book with a blood red title.

"Well good luck. I'll see you after the reading at the book signing."

"Okay. Thanks." Monika was a little nervous.

"...So ladies and gentlemen please welcome bestselling author: MONIKA QUELLER." It was Monika's cue.

The audience began to applaud and Monika walked into the room and up to a small stage. At center stage there was a chair and a microphone. Monika did not sit down. She placed her book upon the chair and adjusted the microphone. She preferred to stand when she did a reading. Picking up her book, she addressed the waiting audience.

"Thank you. It's good to be here. I want to thank you all for coming out and being interested in the book. I hope you enjoy the reading." Monika was brief. She was nervous and wanted to get right into the reading. She felt a little alone and isolated here, far away from California. She opened her book and found the section about San Francisco. She hoped by reading from this part she would feel, at least in her thoughts, closer to home. She took in a breath, and began to read:

... *"Soaring high above San Francisco looking to the north beyond the Bay area was the most magnificent spectacle. The separation between water and the blue heavens was difficult to distinguish. The sun was setting far away into the fine line of horizon between sky and ocean. The water was calm and yet majestic. From this height a few tiny whitecaps speckled throughout the ocean. The water was mirror-like and reflected the brilliance of the day's end. The evening sky colors were incredible in their variety of red, yellow, and violet hues. The sight was heavenly. From far out into the ocean, a giant billowing white mass was gently surfing over the water towards the city. The mountainous land funneled the white mist along its coast and on through the Golden Gate Bridge. Gradually the mist flowed over the bridge and on into the inner bay. The city on its high peaks was surrounded by a soft white. The red spires of the Golden Gate pierced through the white, but that was all that could be seen of its structure. The Bay area was now blanketed by the white mist and tucked in for the night. The land and buildings amidst it seemed to represent a magical kingdom high in the clouds of a make believe world..."*

As she was reading a latecomer entered the room and quietly found a seat near the back. It was the young man from the hotel. Monika momentarily looked up as she read to see who it was and then, without a pause, continued her reading.

●

The reading had gone well and Monika was sitting at a large table autographing copies of her book for those of the audience who wanted signed copies. There was a line-up in front of the table. Monika enjoyed this part of 'authoring'. It gave her the chance to meet one-on-one with her readers and hear their comments. Bob and Gatten were with her, standing off to the side and watching over her.

Gradually the line diminished and there was one person left. It was the young man.

"Hi. Would you mind signing my book?" He looked right into Monika's eyes.

Monika remembered him as the latecomer. "Of course. Who would you like it signed to?"

"Andrew Ambrose."

The name sounded familiar, but Monika couldn't place the reason why. "Is that you?"

"Yes."

"Your name sounds familiar." Monika was asking another non-verbal question through her gestures as she spoke.

Andrew did not answer but shrugged.

Monika took his book and signed on the dedication page and then handed it back to him.

There was an awkward pause as she handed it back to him. She sensed that he wanted something else but was too nervous to ask. Before Monika could ask him if there was anything else, Bob interrupted.

"We're holding a reception in the hotel in an hour. I have a few things to do here with Craig. Would you mind waiting for me?"

Monika turned and faced Bob. "Would you mind if I walked back and met you there? I need the break."

"Are you sure?"

"Yes. It will relax me."

"Well, just follow the boardwalk along the shoreline and it will lead you right back to the hotel. It's about a ten minute walk from here."

"Thanks." Monika turned back to Andrew, but he had gone. She felt bad for being rude and not saying good-bye to him.

Having finished her signing she said her good-byes to those that were nearby and strolled outside.

●

The afternoon was sunny. The water of the lake was calm. A light warm breeze was blowing. Monika was glad she had decided to walk back to the hotel. This was the break she needed to clear her head from the celebrity of the reading and ride out the adrenaline rush that always carried her through the performance.

The sidewalk along the lake was full of people enjoying a late Sunday afternoon walk with their family and friends. Interspersed along the sidewalk were benches with people sitting, talking, smoking or just taking in the view of the harbor and the many sailboats that were passing by.

A little farther out in the harbor, closer to the long thin island that protected the harbor from the open lake, was a regatta of sailing dinghies. Monika stopped and sat on a vacant bench to spend a few quiet moments before heading back to the hotel and the party. She did not realize that amongst the crowd on the sidewalk the young man from the reading was following her.

Monika leaned back into the bench, closed her eyes and took in the warmth of the sun.

"Excuse me, Miss Queller." The male voice startled her.

Monika opened her eyes and was momentarily blinded by the bright sun. She raised her hand to act as a visor and attempted to see who was talking to her. Before her was the hard-to-make-out image of a man. Monika became nervous.

"Do I know you?" she asked as her eyes adjusted to the brightness.

The man moved and blocked the sun from her eyes. Slowly he came into better view.

"Oh…you're the guy from the reading?"

"Yes. Andrew. Andrew Ambrose. Do you mind if I join you for a moment?" He was very soft spoken and Monika felt a tinge of attraction to him. She felt less threatened but was still on guard.

"Sure. Go right ahead."

Andrew sat down next to her and stared out over the harbor. Monika felt a little awkward and wondered what he wanted, but she did not feel in any danger.

Andrew was a good-looking man. He had thick, longish brown hair and dressed casually but neatly. He had welcoming warm hazel eyes, and a boyish smile. They sat in silence for a few moments.

"What can I do for you?" Monika finally broke their silence.

Andrew hesitated and abruptly told her, "I need your help."

"Help? Me? What for?" Monika was surprised. She had thought he was just nervous and wanted to ask her out. Something she had decided she would say yes to. He seemed nice and it would be good to have company.

"Did you get a news clipping last night?"

"News clipping?" Monika began to make the connection. " Ambrose. Ted Ambrose."

"My father."

Monika suddenly understood that this was the son. "Oh. I'm so sorry." She felt sad for Andrew.

"Thanks."

They were silent again.

"Did you slide that under my hotel room door?" Monika wanted to verbally confirm.

"Yes."

After another brief pause Monika inquired, "Why? Why me?"

"I thought you might be able to help. Here." Andrew pulled a piece of folded paper out of his shirt pocket. "Look at this." He handed it to Monika.

'MAN FOUND SHOT.' It was a Toronto newspaper clipping dated three days ago. Monika quickly glanced over the short article. Another man, Rosen, had been killed in exactly the same way as Andrew's father—a single shot to the center of the head—and found in his car in the parking lot at his place of work. He was a vice president of ABM computing, the world's largest personal computer company.

"Odd isn't it?" Andrew noticed Monika's unspoken comparison to the two separate killings.

"So. What are you telling me?"

"Two weeks ago my father, he was a personal courier, goes to meet this guy Rosen for a pick up—meets him in a hotel, signs for the package and turns up dead in the first class lounge at the airport. One week later Rosen turns up dead— same shot to his head in his car at work. The police rule both cases the result of two separate and unconnected robberies, because the bullets don't come from the same gun. It's only a coincidence that they both were shot in the head. They have no leads and don't seem very interested in working the case very hard."

"I'm sorry about your father, but how can I help? Why come to me?" Monika didn't understand why Andrew was telling her all this.

"The only way I'm going to find out who murdered my dad is to find out for myself."

"But that's a police job. Not yours. It could be dangerous."

"As far as I can tell, the police are only going through the motions on this one. Unless I can uncover some more proof, they will never solve the case."

"So why come to me?"

"I read your book. You write about real events. I thought you might help and in return get a story out of it."

Monika laughed. "Well, my publisher is asking me about another book, but I don't normally put myself in danger to write one."

"There's no danger. I just need you to ask some questions."

"Questions?"

"I've done some preliminary investigations. ABM is developing voice imprint encryption for the internet. They have developed a way to make transactions on the internet completely secure using a combination of voice imprinting and pro-gramming. They have developed a new chip that will enable their encryption to work securely without any possibility of hackers breaking in. It's the breakthrough that will turn the internet into the real-time active technology that it has as yet not been able to become. It will be worth billions not only to business transactions, but particularly to the financial and media industries."

"I don't understand." Monika was a little lost.

"I think Rosen was selling ABM out and was offering the chip."

"And your father?"

"Got caught in the middle. He was the innocent party. Merely the courier of the chip. He didn't even know what he was delivering."

"So who killed him?"

"I think it was someone at ABM."

"Why?"

"Somehow they found out about Rosen."

"And got the chip back."

"And got rid of the witnesses."

"That's pretty hard to believe. Why would they take such a risk?"

"From what I can tell, ABM has put everything on the line for this one. If someone else develops this technology and makes it available before they do, it's game over."

"So they will do anything to protect themselves and assure their interests."

"Yes."

"But how can you prove this?" Not that Monika was offering her help, but she was curious how Andrew could find any evidence that would help him corroborate his theory. Evidence that the police would be able to use.

"How many murders are clean single shot hits?"

"What do you mean?"

"My father and Rosen were professional jobs."

"Can you prove it?"

"Not yet. But there must be a file somewhere in ABM."

"File?"

"Yes. A corporation like that would have files on everything."

"Maybe. But they would be kept very secret."

"Yes. That's why I think we should have a look in ABM's CEO's office and see what we can find."

"We?"

"Actually you." Andrew didn't give Monika a chance to respond. He hurriedly added. "You could arrange a meeting with their CEO. His name is Arthur Kazinski. Let them know who you are. Say that you were writing a new mystery involving the computer industry and wanted to ask some questions regarding the industry. You know, the usual thing."

"Then what?"

"Have a look around."

"How can I do that with him there?"

"Get him to show you around the plant. I can go up and sneak into the office and have a look around. By the time you finish your tour I'll be long gone."

"And what if you don't find anything?"

"Then that will be it. All I need is a few hours of your time. There won't be any danger," Andrew was pleading.

Monika silently considered Andrew's proposition.

"What if he doesn't agree to meet with me?"

"Then that's it."

"Or if he doesn't take me on a tour of the plant?"

"Same thing."

"What if you get caught?"

"We never had this conversation and I've never met you in my life. You can go on back to Los Angeles and forget we ever met." Andrew became hopeful.

"When do you want to do this?" Monika was considering the possibilities. She did need a new story. If this all worked out, the publicity would be great for the release of any new book. It seemed to her an enticing proposal.

"Tuesday or Wednesday. You could try to set it up tomorrow."

They did not speak for a few minutes. Monika gazed out into the harbor. The idea of this adventure definitely appealed to her. There did not seem to be much danger involved on her part. If it didn't work out, there was nothing lost and if it did, it would be the beginnings of a great story. She drew in a deep breath and made up her mind.

"I'll phone and see if I can arrange a meeting. No promises. If he agrees, then we'll go for it. If not, then it's over and done with. I don't want any more involvement."

"Yes that's…" Andrew was pleased.

"And we don't know each other." Monika interrupted and reinforced their understanding.

"Thank you. It will all work out. I won't let anything happen to you." Andrew leaned over and hugged Monika.

Monika smiled. She felt happy that Andrew was so cheerful. She privately wondered if she had done the right thing by getting involved with this perfect stranger.

"How can I contact you?" Monika asked as they broke from their hug.

"I'll call you tomorrow afternoon at your hotel. Say two o'clock?"

"Okay."

Monika suddenly remembered the party that was being thrown for her at the hotel. She checked her watch. She had fifteen minutes.

"Look I've got to go. I've got some people waiting for me." Monika stood up and threw out her hand to say good-bye. "I'll talk to you tomorrow."

"Here. You'll need ABM's number." Andrew offered Monika a piece of paper. "I've written the number. Ask for Arthur Kazinski."

Monika took the paper from Andrew and tucked it safely in her purse.

"'Til tomorrow then."

She turned and walked away down the board-walk towards the hotel. Andrew watched her. She quickly became lost in the crowd.

Chapter 5

Monika arrived back at the hotel just in time. Bob was standing inside the main lobby entrance as she came through the revolving doors.

"There you are. I was worried that you'd gotten lost. Everybody's here."

"Oh." Monika was a little out of breath and covered for herself. "I lost track of time. I found a nice little bench by the water and ..."

"Did you want to freshen up?"

"No. I'm fine."

Bob led the way. They walked down the corridor past the shops to a wide curved tan carpeted staircase and went up to the floor above. This was the mezzanine level. There was the sound of music and a party coming from one of the rooms. Bob walked to the first set of double doors and opened them as he and Monika entered. The noise from inside bellowed out.

The room was packed with people, most of whom were quite formally dressed. Everyone was chatting, drinking and making the rounds. There was the sound of a live jazz trio, which Monika quickly located on the far side of the room. There was a bar to their immediate right, which was busy serving the party, and straight ahead the most inspiring view of the harbor and lake. It was really a first class event.

Monika was a bit taken aback that this type of a party was being thrown in her honor. She had expected something on much less grand a scale. She had not realized how much a celebrity she had become. For her Canadian publisher to throw such an impressive bash they must think her quite an up and coming protégé. Bob escorted Monika into the crowd and began the introductions to everyone they met.

Gradually Monika and Bob made their way over to the bar, where Bob got Monika a glass of champagne, but nothing for himself.

"So what do you think?" he asked above the noise.

"It's very nice. Do you guys do this for all your authors?"

"Just the bestsellers." Bob smiled. "Is something wrong? You seem a little preoccupied." He sensed that Monika was a little distant. She was not as outgoing as she was earlier at the reading.

"No, just a little worn." She smiled and perked herself up. "Well maybe there is something. It's not much really. Just a little problem."

"What?"

"When I was sitting on the bench I came up with a story line for another mystery."

"If it's as good as OBSESSION, that will make us all very happy. What's the problem?"

"I wanted to use the computer industry as the backdrop of the story, say ABM, set in Toronto, exposing the corruption of power and its influences after a couple of murders, but I don't know much about the computer business. I was wondering how I might take advantage of my few days here and do some research."

"Any idea of a title?" Bob was fascinated.

"EMERALD CITY."

"Sounds good. Actually you've asked the right guy."

"Really?"

"The CEO of ABM sits on our company's Board of Directors. And he's a fan."

"A fan?" This was quite a stroke of luck. Monika was flattered. It certainly would make things a lot easier.

"Yes. In fact..." Bob searched through the crowd. "There, over there..." Bob discreetly pointed across the room. "See the man between those two woman?"

Monika followed Bob's pointing finger.

"The clean shaven one with red hair?" Monika queried.

"Yes. That's him. Arthur Kazinski."

"He looks a little young to be so powerful."

"Yes. He's very goal-oriented and had a very meteoric rise to the top. I wish I had his savvy." Bob made no attempt to disguise his envy. "Here. Let's go and meet him."

"No, I couldn't." Monika pretended to be shy but it was really fear that held her. Once she met him, there would be no turning back from her plans with Andrew.

"Well, he wants to meet you. I've been told to make certain that I introduce you. It's because of him that this…" he indicated the party, "is so lavish."

Monika drank down her champagne and put the empty glass on a table. "Okay. Let's go."

With Bob in the lead, they made their way over. Monika couldn't help thinking how different Kazinski was from her expectations. She had imagined him to be a much older man in much less good condition. This man was young and exuded power. He also had a penetrating keen glint in his eyes, and he had noticed her before they were half-way towards him. It was as if he had a sixth sense which had alerted him to her presence and purpose. He broke from his conversation with the two woman and stared directly into Monika's eyes. Monika felt intimidated. This was a ladies man and he was interested in more than her books.

"Mr. Kazinski. Monika Queller." Bob said as they came together.

"Ms. Queller." Kazinski was composed as he greeted Monika. He confirmed the subtle sexual undertone that only Monika had so far noticed. He was very aware of the ears around him in the room and would not foolishly give himself away.

"Mr. Kazinski. Thank you for such a lovely party."

"No. Thank you for writing such a gripping book. You are far more striking than your picture."

"Thank you." Monika was a little uncomfortable. This was the man that Andrew believed was behind his father's death.

"Can we expect another one soon?" Kazinski inquired.

"Well actually sir, Ms. Queller was hoping you could be of help to her in that regard." Bob saw the opportunity and took advantage of it.

"Me? Ms. Queller. How can I help? I am not a writer." He laughed, which cued the two women to politely follow suit.

Monika decided to probe carefully.

"Well. I'm writing a mystery set here and using

the computer industry as the backdrop. I'd like to model it after ABM but need to do some research."

"Bob is right. I can help. I run ABM."

"Oh. Would it be too much to request a couple of hours of your time to ask some questions?" Monika became subservient in tone, which was subtly in response to Kazinski's own non-verbal innuendo. Monika would play this card until she got what Andrew needed.

"I can do better than that. Why not come to ABM tomorrow morning to see the operation and meet some real 'nerds'," he joked, "and then have dinner with me later?"

"Oh that would be great." Monika was indeed pleased.

"That's settled then. I'll send a car over for you at ten o'clock."

Monika smiled, "I'll be ready."

"If you'll excuse me. We'll talk more tomorrow. Monika. Bob." Kazinski shook their hands in turn and then, arm in arm with the two women, crossed the room and left the party.

"His girlfriends?" Monika remarked to Bob.

"Assistants / bodyguards."

Monika nodded her head doubtfully.

"It seems you made a good impression."

"Yes." Monika did not let on anything else. "Thanks for your help."

"Any time. Now let's get back to the party."

The rest of the evening was spent being introduced to all the local people of importance in the media and book business. Bob had remained next to Monika all night. She had appreciated him being there to 'protect' her from the 'fans'.

It was not until the party was over, and Monika had been escorted back to her room by Bob and then left alone, that she realized what had happened. She had no way of communicating with Andrew to let him know of her success in setting up a meeting with Kazinski, or the time she would be at ABM. She had to try and locate him by phone.

Picking up the phone from the center table in the sitting room, Monika dialed directory assistance. The phone rang twice and was answered by a female operator.

"Directory assistance. For what city?"

"Toronto and area. Ambrose, A."

There was a short silence as the operator punched in the name.

"I show no listing for an A. Ambrose."

"Oh. What about T?"

Again silence while the operator searched.

"The number is: 905-555-0328." It was a computer voice that gave the number. "Thank you for using Bell Canada."

Monika pressed the button to disconnect and immediately punched in the number that the operator had given her. The phone rang twice at the other end and then was interrupted by a message.

"The number you have reached is not in service. Please check the directory or…"

It was an automated reply. Obviously the phone had been disconnected after Andrew's father's death.

Monika hung up the phone and sat down. Things were now very complicated. She wondered what she was going to do. She could not cancel the meeting. She was not sure if cancelling might raise suspicions. She had no basis for this concern. It was just a feeling she had. Something inside her told her not to take any chances—not to do anything that might, no matter how remote the possibility, cause complications. No matter what, she resolved, she would have to go through with the meeting and take advantage of any opportunity that presented itself while she was there. Maybe Andrew would call earlier than they had agreed. She hoped that he would. If he hadn't called before she left in the morning, she would leave a message with the front desk for him.

It had been a busy day. Monika was tired and a little intoxicated. She lay down to rest a moment before getting ready for bed. The sofa was soft and welcoming. She gave herself up to the comfort it provided and fell asleep.

Chapter 6

Monika awakened early the next morning. The brightness of the light coming through her hotel room window had prevented her from sleeping in. She had showered, dressed and ordered room service. It was 9:45 AM. She had not heard from Andrew and could not wait any longer for his call. She thought of using the hotel stationery that she had found in one of the desks in the room, but decided against a written note. She would leave a short verbal message at the front desk. Realizing the time, she hurried out of the room and headed down the hall for the elevator. She was in luck. The elevator arrived within moments of her depressing its call button.

As she rode down the elevator, Monika admired the view—it helped to distance herself from the apprehension that was growing inside her. She worried about what she was going to do once she arrived at ABM. She hoped that she would think of something; some sort of plan of action before she got there. She had to take advantage of this opportunity. There would probably not be another chance to get into Kazinski's office so easily. This was perfect timing. She should have been prepared for this eventuality. She wished she had gotten Andrew's number.

At the main floor, Monika headed for the front desk. The hotel was not as busy as it had been on Saturday and Sunday. She walked up to the desk clerk.

"Good morning. I have to go out for the morning but I am expecting a call. Could I leave a message for my caller?"

"Certainly, Ma'am. Who is the message for?"

"Andrew Ambrose."

The clerk wrote down the name on the message memo pad. "And the message?"

"Meeting this morning at 10:30."

The clerk completed his writing and verified the message by repeating it to Monika. "Meeting this morning at 10:30?"

"Yes. Thank you." Monika hoped that Andrew would get the message in time. "Oh and I'm expecting a car from ABM Computer."

"Yes Ma'am. Just tell the concierge at that table." The clerk indicated the table across from the front desk and adjacent to the main entrance.

"Thanks." She turned away and crossed over to the concierge's table.

"Good morning, Ma'am. Do you need a cab?" an older white-haired gentleman in a hotel uniform asked as Monika arrived in front of his table.

"No. I'm Monika Queller and a car from ABM Computer is being sent to pick me up."

"Yes Ma'am. It's just arrived. Follow me."

The concierge came around and escorted Monika to the revolving doors of the entrance. Once outside the entrance, Monika waited on the sidewalk of the covered drive while the concierge beckoned to a large black limousine that was waiting several yards away. The limousine sprang to life and pulled up in front of them. The concierge opened the rear passenger door.

"This is your ride, Ma'am. Have a nice day."

Monika thanked him and gave him a five dollar tip before she got into the limousine.

"Thank you very much." The concierge took the tip and helped Monika in, closing the door behind her.

The limousine was richly laid-out in tan leather. Monika sat back in its roomy compartment and took in the sights of the drive. The chauffeur never spoke to, or bothered her as he focused upon his task of delivering her to ABM on time.

The limousine quickly drove down the driveway and turned out of the covered entrance into the bright light of day. It continued down the street and then turned onto a ramp that led up to the same expressway that she had arrived on two days ago. Soon they were riding up above the ground with a clear view of both the city to the north and the lake and harbor, to the south. It was Monika's first opportunity to view more of the city. It was very pretty, with its modern architecture and green vegetation evenly scattered throughout.

The limousine followed the expressway to another highway that was situated in a treed river valley and headed northward. All that Monika could now see was the green of the trees that surrounded the rolling valley. The buildings of the city were hidden behind thick green foliage.

It was not a very long journey and the roads were not at all busy. Within ten minutes of leaving the hotel, the limousine pulled off the highway and headed west on a secondary city road. They were still within the city limits by the look of the surrounding high rises, but it was a part of the city that was situated away from the downtown core and next to this valley. In the distance to her left, about what she guessed was ten miles away, rising over the skyscrapers of the downtown corridor, was the Tower.

Closer and straight ahead, just to the right of the

road they were traveling, there was a one story red brick building. The building spread out over the whole southwest corner of an approaching intersection. It was an old building and stood out amongst all the other more recently constructed high rise office structures that were nearby. There was a large sign atop the building—**ABM**. The letters were large and shone like gold in the sunlight.

The limousine turned right at the intersection and then left into the driveway of ABM. Monika felt a sudden shiver of nervousness as the car pulled up in front of the building and stopped. The driver quickly got out of the car and opened the passenger door to allow her to get out at the main entrance.

"Thank you," Monika acknowledged the chauffeur as she got out.

"You're welcome, Miss. Go straight in. You're expected."

The chauffeur closed the door and stepped forward to open the door to ABM. She passed through and thanked him again.

"Monika. You made it." Kazinski was inside the reception area. "I had the driver call me to let me know you were on your way."

He was in dress pants, a white shirt with gold cuff links and a dark patterned tie. Much more casual than their meeting last night. He was standing in the center of the reception area in front of the entrance.

The reception area was a 'T' junction. Three corridors which led to various parts of the building conjoined there. There were no windows other than the ones facing out in the reception area. Three rows of yellowing fluorescent lights lit the corridors, each running down the center of their respective ceilings. There were doors along the corridors that led to various offices. There was no one else visibly around. It was dingy looking.

Monika was surprised at the appearance of the reception area, and the condition of the building. It was not as plush as she thought it would be nor was there evidence of any type of security or surveillance. The structure reminded her of an old New York City textile factory. She had expected a more computer-designed modular modern building, richly decorated in the art deco of science fiction, from the world's biggest manufacturer of cutting-edge technology; not an out of date middle-of-the-road structure like this one.

Kazinski noticed her observation. It was one that most people made upon visiting ABM for the first time. He enjoyed seeing the reaction. It allowed him to size up a visitor or, more importantly, a businessman, giving him an upper hand and putting him a step ahead before they even started to do business. With Monika, it was an insight that would allow him to better play her to his own advantage.

"We're very relaxed here. Like a big family. We don't spend a lot of time or money on appearances and secretaries. It helps us to work together better and keep a competitive edge. We've been here a long time and haven't changed much. Other than Rosemary," he indicated a young stereotypical bleached blonde receptionist seated behind a counter, "we all take our own calls and arrange our own schedules and greet our own visitors. It seems to work out."

"Thank you for the car." Monika did not comment on ABM's philosophy. A philosophy that would make it easier for Andrew to slip by and look around in Kazinski's office.

"Why don't we go into my office." Kazinski ushered Monika along with him. He put his arm around her waist making his preliminary pass at her as they walked.

They went about twenty feet up the hallway to the left of the reception area. Kazinski opened the first door they came to, again on their left.

"After you," he said as he ushered her inside.

Monika entered. The decor inside was not what she expected. It was the complete opposite of the outside hall and reception area. The office was large. A computer monitor and keyboard sat upon an expensive looking old style wood desk. Adjacent to a large calendar / blotting pad, which protected the desk's highly polished surface, sat a modern touch-tone phone.

Behind the desk was a large double glazed window with a horizontal white venetian blind. The blind was open and allowed one to overlook a small forested area which Monika had not seen from the front of the building.

The walls of the office were dark and lined with rich wood paneling. There were chairs on both sides of the desk, and a couch along the right-hand wall of the office. Two large black filing cabinets were on the opposite wall.

"Please sit," Kazinski directed. He went around to his chair on the other side of the desk as Monika made herself comfortable.

Monika was discreetly searching the room, though she wasn't sure what she was looking for. She was very nervous. She hoped Andrew got her message. Maybe she should phone the hotel and check.

"Would you mind if I call the hotel? I'm expecting a call," Monika asked.

"No. Please." Kazinski offered her the phone and sat back in his chair, watching her. There was a glint in his eyes.

Monika took out a pad of paper from her purse and keyed in the number. The phone rang three times.

"Weston Hotel."

"Hi. Are there any messages for Monika Queller?"

"Just a minute, Ma'am." The clerk put her on

hold.

Monika smiled bashfully at Kazinski during the wait for the clerk to check.

"Hello." The clerk came back on line.

"Yes."

"No Ma'am. No messages."

Monika's heart fell.

"Thank you." She hung up the phone and sat back in her chair.

"Everything alright?" Kazinski questioned.

"Yes. No calls." Monika was concerned.

'What am I going to do?' she thought to herself. Should she just continue with the interview and the tour, or find a way to search through the filing cabinets and desk in the office?

Monika was feeling increasingly uncomfortable. She had not expected that this might happen. She had thought that, under these circumstances, she would have just forgotten about helping Andrew and merely carried on—but there was something about Kazinski that intrigued her; something about him that also made her dislike him. She wanted to help Andrew any way she could if it meant exposing that side of Kazinski.

Kazinski sat like a cat regarding its prey. He looked very self-assured as he peered across the desk at Monika. He noticed her discomfort, but attributed it to desire. He liked this young woman and would continue to prey upon her. There wasn't anyone that he couldn't seduce. He sensed that

Monika was a little more of a challenge. She was shy, beautiful and yet very intelligent. His normal approach would not work here. First he needed to gain her confidence. He decided to be charming and helpful today. He would personally escort her around the plant. Later, after they met for dinner, he would make his move.

"So what would you like to know?" he began.

Monika nervously readied her notepad and, with pen in hand, the interview began.

"Do you mind if I take some notes?"

"No. Not at all." Kazinski was flattered that a pretty bestselling author like Monika would want to write his words down.

"I should start with you. How did you start off in computers?"

Kazinski began a short summary of his early years while Monika jotted down notes. It was clear to her, as he spoke, that he had been a 'nerdy' type in his youth. He had been far more bright and technically-oriented than most of his peers and fit easily into that outcast group. Though he enjoyed being different, he had been emotionally hurt by the labels put on him and others like him. Though he did not say so in words, Monika read between the lines.

His parents had come from the middle class and pushed him to succeed. He had been advanced through school and was given every opportunity by them to be exposed to all those things that most young people disliked, but he had enjoyed, such as the opera and theater.

Eventually he found his way into university at the age of sixteen. Being too young to be interesting to the woman on campus, he again was an outcast. The only place he made friends, probably because of his age, was in the new discipline of computer science.

Monika felt a little sorry for Kazinski as she listened to his story. It must have been hard to be so bright and yet socially have nothing in common with the majority of the students around him. This explained to her his current personality, at least his womanizing. After Kazinski finished his life story, she continued to ask her questions.

They continued for about twenty minutes. Kazinski had been opening up to her and did not appear to be on guard or holding anything back. He was very comfortable with her questions and eager to answer them.

"What about the future of personal computing? Where does ABM see it going?" Monika, having acquired enough background information to help her with any characterization in the proposed story, branched into another line of questions. Before he could answer, the office phone rang.

"Excuse me." Kazinski picked up the phone. "Kazinski." He spoke in a stern tone, not at all like the warm manner he had been using with Monika. This was an insight into his business personality. He was a clever man and played whatever part required, in any given situation, in order to succeed. He was like a chameleon, constantly changing as he went from scenario to scenario.

"Yes. I'll be right there." Kazinski's mood was altered by the call. He looked apologetically over to Monika, who was waiting for the answer to her last question.

"Sorry. Duty calls. Something is wrong in the plant and they need me. Would you mind if I left you for a few moments? I am sorry for the interruption." He sat awaiting her permission.

Monika, who had been getting involved with the questioning, suddenly realized that this was her chance to help Andrew. While Kazinski was out of the room she could rummage around. She thought there would be ample time in his absence to thoroughly search through the filing cabinets and his desk.

"No. By all means. I'm grateful that you are giving me so much time. I can go over my notes and organize my thoughts."

"Fine." Kazinski smiled and stood up. "I won't be long." He crossed the room and opened his office door.

"There's no rush." Monika turned in her chair. Her skirt had risen up quite high from sitting and revealed much more of her. Kazinski glanced at her lovely long legs. Monika feigned shyness, realizing her exposure and the direction of his stare.

"I'll be waiting." She smiled and implied a double meaning. She too could be chameleon-like if it suited her need. She wanted to reassure Kazinski that he need not rush; that she was still a sexual possibility to him; that she understood and would wait.

Kazinski smiled and looked her in the eyes; then he left the office, closing the door after him.

Monika couldn't believe her luck. There was no time to waste. After waiting to be sure that he was gone, she got up and carefully cracked open the office door. She peeked through the crack. The hall was empty. Carefully closing the door, she saw that there was a locking mechanism in the handle. She twisted it, locking the door. She felt a little more secure.

Immediately she crossed to the filing cabinets and began to rifle through them drawer by drawer. There were all sorts of files. She was not sure what to look for as she thumbed through; all the time she was half-listening for Kazinski's return. She was beginning to perspire from her apprehension. With each new drawer that she examined and did not find anything of particular interest, she became increasingly agitated. The searching, though it lasted only seconds, seemed to be taking forever. It was frustrating that it was bringing no results. She wondered how long she had before Kazinski came back.

The filing cabinets bearing no fruit, Monika turned her attention to Kazinski's large wood desk. She hurried across the room and began to go through the desk cupboard on the left side. She found nothing except three telephone books and a yellow pages. The books fell out onto the floor and made a noise as she opened the desk door. She froze in place thinking that the noise would be heard but, after a short pause, realized that it hadn't and quickly put the books back in the cupboard.

Next she slid open the central drawer. It was full of pens, pencils and paper clips, but nothing else of interest. Monika was very concerned that she was running out of time and was not going to find anything. She had to hurry. Kazinski might reappear at any second.

She turned her attention to the three remaining drawers on her right. She pulled open the top drawer. It was not a deep drawer and was full of stationery. She shuffled through the paper, but found nothing.

Closing the top drawer she slid half open the middle one. It also was not very deep. It appeared to be empty. She opened the drawer fully and discovered a small caliber hand gun in the back. The gun was shiny and well maintained. It was placed where it could be readily grabbed by Kazinski's right hand, and easily pointed and fired. Monika was taken aback and withdrew her hands, placing them closer to herself and away from the weapon. The reality of the danger of Kazinski became very evident. The gun confirmed to her the jeopardy she would be in if she were discovered snooping through his office. She must hurry.

She closed the drawer and proceeded to the lower one. It would not open. She pulled on its handle a couple of times, but it still did not open. Monika crouched down to better examine the locked drawer. Somehow she had to get it open. It was the only locked item in the room and might be the one to reveal to her something of interest for Andrew.

She grabbed a metal letter opener from atop the desk and slid it into the crack of the drawer. She began to twist and pry at the lock as she pulled on the handle of the drawer. She was beginning to panic. She felt that time was running out; that Kazinski would return at any moment. She pulled harder as she pried at the locking mechanism, being careful not to do any damage to the visible part of the desk.

Unexpectedly the blade of the letter opener snapped and the drawer opened under her force. Monika picked the broken blade out of the drawer and placed it along with its handle in her purse. She could not take the chance of disposing of it here in the office where it might be discovered.

This drawer was deeper than the upper two. It contained row upon row of computer plastic floppy disks and CD ROMs. Monika felt that she had found something of interest. She began rummaging through. She still was not sure what she was looking for. The disks were all carefully labeled and catalogued, but nothing struck her as an item she might be in search of. She went through the disks. They all seemed to be samples of one sort or another of the programs that were developed by ABM. Each disk had the ABM logo stamped upon it and typed names of the disks. The CDs were similarly mass-marketed samples. Everything was very similar. Nothing seemed to stand out.

She continued to flip through the drawers contents, becoming very desperate as her time ran out. As she came to the last few CDs she found something different. There were two RCDs (recordable CDs). These were not mass produced but were made in-house for personal private use. Monika knew this media—she used it to back up her own files at home. She had recently bought a recordable CD unit with the advance of her royalties from OBSESSION.

She stopped at these CDs. Her intuition told her that she had found something. There was no time to think. She took the two RCDs out of the drawer and stood up. She considered for a moment what was contained on them and where she might hide them. Her purse was too obvious. Quickly she raised up her skirt and placed the RCDs in her panties. They were cool against her skin. She pulled her skirt back down and straightened her clothing, making sure that the CDs did not show. The RCDs would be safe there until she got out of ABM.

Closing the drawer, Monika manipulated the lock back into its original position by prying it shut using the broken blade of the letter opener. Once shut, she placed the blade back into her purse, straightened her skirt again, crossed the room to the door to unlock the mechanism and returned to sit down where she had been when Kazinski had left. She drew in a couple of deep breaths and wiped away the beads of perspiration that had developed upon her forehead with a facial tissue from a box on the desk. She was pleased with herself and hoped she could carry off the rest of the meeting without giving herself away or raising any suspicions. She prayed that Kazinski would be a few minutes longer, which would allow her time to compose herself. Her heart was racing.

About five minutes after Monika's successful search, the door to the office opened and an apologetic Kazinski reappeared.

"I'm sorry it took so long."

Monika stood up. "No. No. It wasn't that long at all. I realize you're busy."

She readied herself to imply that she was getting set to leave.

"Maybe we should do this another time, if you're busy now?" She would be happy if she could cut this short and get out.

"Not at all. It was just a minor problem and it's all solved now. How about that tour I promised you?"

"Well, only if you're sure," Monika tested.

"I'm all yours." Kazinski opened his arms as he spoke. "Why don't we go now. We can finish the questions over dinner tonight, say eight. I'll send the car to pick you up."

Monika was in a difficult situation. She did not particularly want to have dinner with him, but it would be the normal thing to do under the circumstances and she did not want to upset Kazinski or make him suspicious of her motives for wanting to come to ABM. She wanted to keep her options open just in case.

"Okay." Monika timidly agreed as she moved towards the door and spoke. She felt the hard RCDs pressing against her with her every movement.

Kazinski led the way. The two left the office and went along the corridor back in the direction of the reception area. They did not stop at reception but walked straight on down the corridor on the other side. All the while Kazinski was chatting with her. Finally they came to a door at the end of the corridor and as they went through it Kazinski started to explain all that they saw.

"This is our main production area. All the components are assembled here, though the parts are all made elsewhere," he said with pride.

They were standing in an anti-room that was separated by a glass partition from the assembly area. From this viewing room the whole production process could be seen. There were lines of conveyor belts and people dressed in white clothing that gave them the look of research scientists and not mere assembly line workers. They wore protective head covering and glasses—even their shoes were covered with the white protective coverings. The room was quite large and spotless. It reminded Monika of an operating room in a large hospital.

"Why all the precautions?" Monika inquired.

"The chips are very sensitive at this stage. We don't like to take any unnecessary risks in exposing them to electrostatic charges and general outside dust contamination. It helps to assure better quality control. Would you like to go in? We can suit up if you like."

"No. It's very interesting, but maybe another time. Is this your whole plant?" Monika thought in a hurry, wanting to appear interested.

"No. There's a whole area for our R & D and programming. But I'm afraid it's a restricted area. Very hush hush."

"So that's where you hide all your secrets," Monika joked.

"Secrets?" Kazinski's tone changed. He was not sure what Monika was implying.

"I mean, all those things that make your computers the best. You know…" Monika innocently covered her comment. Kazinski had no sense of humor. "The next generation and stuff."

Kazinski changed his tone and chuckled. She had meant the usual secrets, nothing else. "Yes. I see what you mean."

There was a slight awkwardness between them. They stood and watched the assembly process for a while.

"Well. I hope this has been of some help, Monika. Is there anything else I can show you?"

"Oh no. This has been great. This will help a lot." Monika was genuine.

"Then let me see you to the car." He guided her out of the viewing room.

Monika cheerfully followed. She would soon be away and safe. She began to feel less stressed. The end was in sight. With her tension reduced, she became a little more talkative with Kazinski on their way back down the hall to the reception area and the waiting limousine. She was pleased with herself for having been so good at pulling the deception off successfully. She hoped that she had found something of use and that Andrew would be happy. She could not wait to load the CDs into her notebook back in her room at the hotel to see what she had found.

Kazinski walked Monika through the reception area and out to the large black company limousine that was still parked out in front and waiting. The chauffeur, who was standing by the car, quickly came over and opened the passenger door when he saw them come out. Kazinski ignored the chauffeur. He helped Monika get in the vehicle and, leaning his head inside, said "I'll see you at eight then."

He pulled back and stood away from the limousine. He had become suddenly more formal. Monika suspected it was because of the chauffeur's presence.

Without saying a word or being acknowledged by Kazinski, the chauffeur closed the door. The dark windows hid Monika from view, but this did not stop Kazinski from staring right at her. From inside, it seemed to Monika that he could still see her even through the dark tint of the window. She felt a shiver run up her from the base of her spine. It was an eerie sensation. She did not like him and was pleased to be almost away from his grasp.

The chauffeur crossed over to his door, opened it, got in and started the limousine. Slowly it pulled ahead. Monika watched as Kazinski turned and went back into the building. She was relieved. She discreetly adjusted the CDs in her underwear and let out a sigh of relief. She smiled to herself. She had done it. She checked the time on her wristwatch: 11:45. She had been there just over an hour. It had seemed much longer.

Chapter 7

Kazinski came back to his office and sat down at his desk. Monika had been a very pleasant distraction, but now there was work that required his immediate attention. He looked forward to this evening and dinner.

On his desk was the morning mail. He picked up the small pile that had been stacked there while he'd been giving Monika a tour of the plant. He thumbed through the envelopes and, after choosing the first one, put the rest down in front of him. He looked to the spot where he always kept his letter opener. The letter opener had been given to him a long time ago by his parents and he had a sentimental attachment to it. It was not in its place. He visually searched the desktop. Not finding the opener, he put down the envelope. It was very strange that the opener was not in its usual place. Kazinski searched the desktop for it again. This time he lifted up and checked around everything upon the desktop, but still did not find it. He was clearly becoming very upset. He sat back to try and remember when he had used it last. This was a method he always applied to finding misplaced objects. He would try to picture the lost item in his mind and then visualize when and where he'd last seen it.

As he sat back in his chair, trying to recall his last memory of the opener, he happened to notice a small imperfection on the bottom drawer of the right side of his desk. He frowned and leaned forward to examine the mark that marred the part of the desk that the drawer slid into. He touched the spot. There was a small flat impression in the finish located centrally above the lock. He was puzzled. He pulled the drawer handle and the lock did its job preventing the drawer from opening. He wondered how his desk had received this mark. It was obviously not caused by the mechanism itself, but something else. He bent closer to better examine the damage. The mark appeared to be fresh. He did not ever recall having seen it there before today. It looked as if someone had tried to pry the drawer open, but who and when?

Taking his keys out of his pants pocket, Kazinski unlocked the drawer and slid it open to its full length. Nothing seemed out of place. Everything was neatly lined up as it should be. Unconsciously he flipped through the section of the CDs and came to an empty spot. Two CDs were missing. Quickly he fanned through the drawer to find the misplaced items. They were not in the drawer. They were definitely missing.

Kazinski thought a moment. Who could have taken them? No one had been in his office… No one… except…Ms. Queller!

The notion struck him that while she had been left alone, she had been prowling around. Not being able to open the locked drawer, she must have pried it open and then taken the CDs.

Kazinski became angry. How could he have been taken in by her? Who was she really? He wondered who she might be working for. She was obviously more than just a mystery writer. Panic set in when he considered her motives. Monika had taken the two CDs that could bring him down. He had to get them back, and quickly. He had to find out who else was behind this scheme.

Sitting back down, Kazinski went into action. He picked up the phone and punched in a number. The phone was answered and he ordered: "Get in here now." Then he hung up the phone. He slammed the drawer shut in a display of his violent nature. "Damn her!"

Within moments of his call there was a knock at his door.

"Come in," Kazinski snapped in an angry tone.

The door opened and two rather large men, who looked like football players dressed in expensive suits, entered.

"Close it." Kazinski meant the door. By their demeanor, they were clearly intimidated by Kazinski's power, even though they physically were much stronger.

One of the men complied with the order and they both came forward and stood in front of the desk.

"Yes sir?" one of the men asked Kazinski.

"My guest here this morning was not who she appeared to be."

"Ms. Queller, sir?" The man who had closed the door did not understand.

"Yes."

"But we checked her out."

"Well you didn't do a very thorough job!" Kazinski threatened. The two men cowered, but did not say anything.

"I want her brought back. Go and get her. She's staying at the Harbor Weston. She has two of my RCDs. Make sure you find them and bring them back with you as well." There was an implied 'or else' to his words.

"Yes sir," both men acknowledged.

"Bring her here."

"Yes sir."

"Now get out!"

The men turned and left the room. They were relieved to be away from Kazinski when he was angry. They had worked for him since the early days and were a part of his security team. They knew from his tone that he meant business and would not tolerate failure.

●

Monika arrived back at her hotel and went straight to her room without stopping at the front desk to see if there were any messages for her. When she got into her room, she lifted up her skirt and reached for the two CDs. She took them out and put them, with her purse, on the table in the sitting room. She then went into her bedroom to the closet to get her notebook, which was in its carry case inside her suitcase. She always traveled with it that way. She did not worry about it being stolen. So far nothing had ever happened to it and she always had back up copies of the files in it.

She got the carry case out of her suitcase and returned to the sitting room where she placed it next to the CDs on the table. As she opened the case and took out the notebook, she thought it quite a coincidence that it was made by ABM.

She opened the notebook and pressed a key. Instantly the computer awoke from its sleep mode. She inserted one of the CDs into the machine and waited 'til it showed up on the screen. An ABM icon appeared. Monika pointed her mouse and double clicked. The CD opened and revealed the names of the files it contained. Monika chose one of the files and double clicked again. This time a message box displayed: 'Enter Password'. She was disappointed. She had hoped that the files were not encrypted. Getting the information from these files was going to be hard. She found herself wishing that James were here. She knew he would have been able to help. She wished he had not let her down.

Monika did not dwell on this thought long. She closed the password request box and tried a few of the other files. They were all encrypted. She ejected the CD and inserted the other. Again she discovered similar encrypted files. Frustrated by this misfortune, she slammed her hands on the table.

"Damn!" she said out loud. She would have to wait for Andrew. Hopefully he could break into the files.

Monika wondered what she should do while she waited for Andrew's call. It was just after twelve noon and he would not be calling 'til two-ish. She was nervous about staying in her room with these CDs. Her intuition was telling her to get out.

As Monika sat back on the sitting room sofa, she had an idea. She could e-mail the CDs to James with a message. Yes, she decided. That was the best thing to do. Then if anything went wrong, James would know, and have the CDs. Though she was angry at him, this was great insurance against any unforeseen development with Kazinski at dinner. Someone else would know about the CDs.

Monika searched through her carry case and took out a long phone wire extension. She plugged the wire into the back of her notebook into the modem slot and then got up to find where the room phone was plugged into the wall. She undid the phone and plugged in the modem. She came back to the notebook and opened up her internet communications program. Once opened, she directed the program to dial a 1-888 number which would connect her to her internet provider. The computer dialed the number. The high-pitched sounds of her modem connecting filled the otherwise silent room.

Up on the screen appeared the home page of her provider. She glanced at her mailbox, but there was no flag next to the icon which would have indicated that she had new mail. She opened a new e-mail document and filled in the address for James. She then wrote a quick note:

"James. Can you get into these attached files? Keep it between us. Most urgent. Monika."

She then instructed the program to attach the files. The program asked to locate the files. Monika identified the first CD and the program quickly began to copy the files and attach them to the e-mail document. When it was finished, she directed the program to attach another file. She ejected the first CD and inserted the second. The program began to upload it and displayed its progress as it had with the previous CD. The whole process took a few minutes, and when it was complete, Monika depressed the send button. The program responded and a dialogue box appeared noting the files had been sent. James would receive the e-mail in seconds. She disconnected from the provider and turned the notebook off. She hoped that he would be checking his mail soon. In the meantime, she would take the CDs and go out. She felt safer to be out of her room, just in case Kazinski had discovered the theft.

Monika undid the modem extension and, after placing the CDs in her purse, put the notebook back into its carry case. She zipped it closed and placed the case on the carpeted floor against the sofa, out of direct view.

●

Kazinski's two men arrived at the hotel at the same time that Monika had completed her e-mail to James and put the notebook away. They pulled up the drive to the main lobby entrance. One man got out and went into the hotel to the front desk to inquire after Monika, while the other stayed with the car.

The hotel was not busy. The man came up to the clerk at the front desk.

"I'm meeting a Ms. Queller."

"Yes sir. Just a minute." The clerk went over to

a message box and came back. "Are you Mr. Ambrose? Mr. Andrew Ambrose?" the clerk asked.

The man was surprised, but did not show his shock. "Yes. I am."

"Ms. Queller left this message." The clerk handed the man the message.

"Thank you," the man said as he took and quickly read the message.

"Is she back yet?" He put the message into his jacket pocket as he questioned the clerk.

"I don't know sir. But you can use the courtesy phone to ring her room. Just dial the room number. It's 1711 South."

The man thanked the clerk and walked away. As he left, another person stepped up from behind for his turn with the clerk.

The man crossed to a table adjacent to the front desk and picked up a courtesy phone. He punched in 1711 S. The phone rang.

●

Monika was still sitting on the sofa when the phone in the bedroom rang. She was startled by its sudden, sharp ring. She realized that she had forgotten to plug the sitting room phone back into the wall jack. She quickly got up and, with phone in hand, went to the wall and plugged the phone back in. The phone in her hand began to ring in unison with the phone in the bedroom. Monika was excited. Maybe this was Andrew calling.

She lifted the receiver up to her ear and said,
"Hello?"

●

The man on the courtesy phone heard Monika's
voice. He hung up the phone without saying a
word. She was back. He would hurry up to her
room and escort her out with him to the waiting
car.

●

"Hello?"
No one answered. Whoever was calling had
hung up the phone after hearing her voice.
Monika placed the receiver back into its cradle
and put the phone down. Every instinct within her
was screaming to get out; that she was in danger
and that the phone call was checking up on her to
see if she was in her room. She suddenly understood.

"Kazinski knows. I've got to get out of here
now." Monika spoke out loud to herself. She
lapsed into this behavior whenever she was alone
and afraid. It helped to reassure her that everything would be alright.

She grabbed her purse from the table and went
to the room door. She peered through the peep
hole. Nobody was outside the door. Nervously,
she decided to open the door and carefully check
to see that the hall was clear. She turned the handle and opened the door. She placed her right eye
to the small crack between the door and jam. She

could see the hallway to her left. Again nobody was there. She tried to look in the other direction. She was not able to see to her right. She hesitated. She then decided that if someone was waiting out there, they would have been in on her after the door was cracked open. She took in a breath and fully opened the door. She stepped out into the hall, closing the door behind her, keeping her attention on the hallway at all times. She walked down the hall to the elevator and pushed the call button.

"What if someone is on the elevator?" she questioned herself. "It would be wiser to take the stairs."

Monika left the elevator and walked further down the hall. She found the stairwell exit and opened the door. She peeked in. Seeing that the way was clear, she stepped in and closed the door behind her.

The stairwell was vacant and barren. Its cement walls were unpainted and grey. It was quite a contrast from the rest of the hotel. Monika's heart was pounding as she began to descend.

●

The elevator rang at Monika's floor seconds after she had started down the stairs. The doors opened and out stepped the man who had made the call to her room from the main lobby. The man checked the room number directions on the wall opposite the elevator as he got out and the doors closed behind him. 1711 was to his left. He went down the hall and found Monika's room.

Stopping outside the door, the man pulled out a gun from inside his jacket holster and knocked with the butt of the gun upon the door.

"Ms. Queller? Room service." He called out in a meek voice.

The man waited but there was no answer. It did not take him long to realize that something was wrong. He checked around the hall to make certain that no one else was nearby and proceeded to break the door down. It was not a difficult task for such a large man. The door lock broke on his third attempt at forcing. He had used the force of his right leg applied against the handle area to kick his way in.

One inside, and with gun drawn, he searched through the rooms. He quickly looked in the closets, bathroom, bedroom and under the bed. Monika was not there. She was gone. His phone call had alerted her. She must have just left.

The man put away the gun and ran out from the room back to the elevator. The indicator above the elevators did not show any movement. She must have taken the stairs.

●

Monika was descending as fast as she could down the stairs. She sensed that she was in danger and that she must hurry. She had gone down several levels but there was still a long way to go.

She was quickly becoming out of breath. The shoes she was wearing were not well-suited to this type of use and were slowing her progress. She stopped to catch her breath. She listened to the sounds within the stairwell. She strained her ears. The sound of her pounding heart, both from her fear and exertion, made it hard to hear. She tried to hold her breath and slow the pounding. She listened.

●

The man found the door to the stairs and opened it. He walked in and let go of the door which slammed closed behind him. He listened for any sound of Monika upon the stairs.

●

Monika heard the sound of a door slamming shut somewhere above in the stairwell. She was being followed. She panicked. There was some-one coming after her. There was no time to waste. She continued her descent. The sound of her heals began to echo throughout the stairwell. She did not care about the noise. It was more important to keep whatever lead she had and get away.

●

The man heard the sound of Monika's quick-ened steps as she escaped down the stairs. He started after her. It sounded like she was not very far ahead of him. He had to catch up with her before she got out of the stairwell and disappeared in the hotel. He leapt forward down the stairs, taking two steps at a time. He did not want to lose her. She would be hard to find if she got away, especially now that she was alerted to her danger.

●

Monika kept up a good pace. She could easily hear the sound of her pursuer as they both raced down level by level. She still had a good lead. She believed that she could make it to the mezzanine level of the hotel and then out into the anonymity of the public to safety. Once out of danger from her pursuer, she could make it out of the hotel. Once out of the hotel, she could find a pay phone and try to make arrangements to meet with Andrew in some safe place. She hoped that Andrew would leave a number where she could reach him when he called.

She continued down the stairs. She was only a couple of floors away from safely making her escape. Dinner with Kazinski was obviously canceled.

Chapter 8

James was just returning from his morning coffee break. He had come into the Los Angeles office early. He had not spoken to Monika since her abrupt departure. He was upset with her for leaving and mad at her for abandoning his car at the airport. He had spent half the day finding and then getting his car from the impound yard near the airport. Fortunately, he was able to use his connections to avoid paying the towing charges. He had had a hard time explaining to his superiors why he had been so late for the surprise meeting that they had called him to on Saturday. That meeting had placed him here in the L.A. office on a case.

James had driven up early this morning to avoid

the Monday morning rush hour traffic coming
north into L.A. from the outskirts of Oceanside.
As well as being angry with her, he was also missing Monika. He felt a longing inside—a persistent
pulling at him to be with her. He wanted the sad
feeling to go away. He needed his fix of her. He
needed to get his mind back on his work. He
wanted to distract his thoughts away from this
yearning, but nothing seemed to work. Only contact with her would calm him, but his ego was
hurt. He was not going to call her. She was wrong,
and had over-reacted. He hoped that he would
hear from her soon.

The downtown L.A. office was situated on the
sixteenth floor of a new skyscraper. The view
from this office was a magnificent exposure south
to the ocean. When James returned to his desk
from getting his coffee, he sat and gazed out over
the vista. He wondered how Monika had done at
her book festival.

James' desk was cluttered. He had only been
there a few hours and there were papers, binders,
and other materials that he was using for research
on his new case assignment. A large monitor, a
mouse and pad for his computer, was situated on
the left side of his grey metal desk. The monitor
displayed a floating digital clock as a screen
saver. The clock melted and reappeared in a
smooth hypnotic motion mesmerizing him further. It was amazing to James how much paper-

work was involved in the 'company', compared to the popular Hollywood depiction of agents in the CIA.

James was wearing a smart, but conservative, suit with a white shirt and a nondescript tie. His shoes were highly polished as per company rules. He looked more like a successful businessman than an enforcer of the law.

As he sat there entranced by the view and the screen saver, he sipped his coffee. It was 9:34:00 AM. Suddenly a voice emanated from the monitor speakers and the screen saver changed to a dialogue box.

"You have mail." It was a cheerful female computer voice notifying him that he had just received e-mail.

He sprang forward. He placed his coffee down on his desk and, using the mouse, double clicked on the dialogue box. Right away his computer launched his communications program and another dialogue box appeared. In the box was written: 'You have one piece of new mail. Would you like to read it now?'

James clicked the 'YES' option and in a couple of seconds the e-mail appeared on screen. James read the message header. It was from Monika and sent about a minute ago. There was a message and two large attachments. He read the message:

'James. Can you get into these two attached files? Keep it between us. Most urgent. Monika.'

It was not the message that James expected. He found its tone flat and emotionless. He was curious why Monika had sent him such a note along with these attached files. It was strange that she would send such large files to him and not a more personal note. He was, however, pleased to have at least had some sort of communication from her. It told him they were still speaking, even if it was a little cool. He clicked on the two attached files and began to download them.

It took several minutes to finish downloading the files. When that was completed, he closed the communications program and turned his attention to the two files. They were labeled ABM 1 and ABM 2. He double clicked on the first. The file opened to a dialogue box that requested the 'Password'. So that was why Monika sent these to him. James understood. Monika wanted him to unencrypt the files using his resources. James was intrigued. What was so important about these ABM files? More importantly, where and how did Monika get them?

James searched his hard drive and launched another program. This was a diagnostic tool that he could use to identify the encryption method used on the ABM files. He sat back, watched the monitor, and waited. After five or so minutes the program had diagnosed the files and identified the encryption method.

"Got ya," James proudly spoke out loud. He

was a whiz at breaking encryptions. It was his specialty and he took great pride in his ability.

Now that he had identified the encryption method, he could methodically go through the file forks and gradually break into the files. It was only a matter of time before the contents of the files were exposed.

Line by line James went through the machine language that was presented before him on the screen. He studied each resource, looking for the particular aspects of it that were causing the encryption. Everything about the files was being presented to him. He viewed each section of the Master Directory Block, and Extents and Catalog Trees. Every item was identified and presented to him to analyze:

Total bytes on Volume   0
Free bytes on Volume   0
Clump size   98,989
First sector in Block Map   2
Volume attributes $2400($0000in vcb).

He spent quite some time going through each line until he achieved some success. Part of the file was invisible. He highlighted the sector and changed a few critical elements of the data. He then clicked 'OPEN' under his file menu and waited. He held his breath in anticipation of his success or failure.

After a few seconds of delay, the file booted up and opened. He had bypassed the password and managed to unencrypt the files.

He grinned. It had been a remarkably simple encryption. He had believed that a company as sophisticated as ABM would have used much more intricate systems.

He began to examine the files. The files contained lists of names, phone numbers, serial and model numbers of particular ABM computers and some of their clones that contained a mother board manufactured by them. It was a curious list. The names were a cross-section of international business and government agencies. Under each of the names was a list of software, their versions and inits used by that organization. It seemed to be a very comprehensive listing of data. He wondered what these lists were and why they had been compiled and then so carefully hidden. They seemed to be registration lists of all new ABM hardware and software users. The earliest version of the ABM operating system on each of these listings was the one issued by ABM last fall.

James continued to read through all the various lists. ABM had computers in every major organization in the world. It was truly a universal company and product. ABM had done an effective job in saturating the marketplace with their computing products. Clearly they had helped, if not started, the revolution to transfer all data from paper to electronic storage. Most, if not all, major organizations either used an ABM product, or were dependent upon electronic storage and retrieval of data from a company that used an ABM system. But these lists were more than just a compilation of ABM's newest customers for warranty purposes. James' instincts told him that there was something more going on here.

He began to compare the lists and the information contained in the two files manually but could not identify anything outstanding. He decided to save the lists in a format that he could analyze. He saved the two files together. They were tremendously large and stretched the capacities of his system. Once the files were saved he began to set up parameters for searching. He started his computer in its search and got up from his desk to get another coffee while he waited for the program to complete its task.

There was something very odd about Monika having obtained these files. ABM would not willingly release such data publicly. James was becoming concerned. If Monika had obtained these files illicitly, she may be in more trouble than she knew. Once he had completed his analysis he would call her at her hotel in 'Emerald City' to check up on her. With this thought in mind, he walked out of the office to get his coffee.

By the time James returned with his coffee, his computer had finished its analysis. He sat down at his desk and began to move his way through the data displayed on his screen with his mouse.

There were many similarities to much of the data that each organization contained, but it was all of the type one would expect to find from a company's client and warranty database. Other than the fact that all these organizations used ABM or an ABM cloned product, there was only one constant they all hand in common. At the end of each list were the two capitalized letters 'RA' followed by a designation of either 'activated', 'not activated' or 'in process'.

James was curious as to what the RA stood for. He sat back in his chair and contemplated the possibilities. It had to be something related to computer technology; something that ABM wanted to keep secret; otherwise they would not have used symbols but the long form of the actual words.

"Ram Available. No," he said out loud. "How would that work with activated or in process?"

He became silent as he continued to think. "Ram Access? No. Random. …Remote?" He became intrigued. "Remote Access? Remote Access activated. Remote Access not activated. Remote ACCESS IN PROGRESS!"

That was it! ABM had remote access availability in their computers. They were accessing data from big business and government. That was it. How smart. No one would know or suspect. Most of the new computers came with a communication package including voice mail systems. More and more organizations as well as individuals left their computers turned on and plugged into the phone lines twenty-four hours a day. In fact, James remembered reading somewhere how ABM actually recommended never unhooking or turning computers off.

'Of course. How simple,' James thought. That made it a lot easier for them. ABM could access this data after-hours via the phone connection. They would have complete access to any data no matter how secret or sensitive as long as it was stored on, or linked to, one of their new computers. The listings on the two files that Monika had sent indicated those organizations ABM had already accessed or were in the process of accessing data from.

The simplicity of the scheme was unbelievable. There would be no way for an organization to be aware that all their data was available and being used for profit by ABM. If such an organization used the encryption software supplied by ABM, it would provide no protection. ABM would have overrides written under the program that only they knew about and could activate. By relying to such an extent on ABM computers, they were helping to undermine themselves. ABM was in a position to have international access to the most import business and government secrets. Since computing was still in its infancy, and most individuals using computers had little knowledge of their actual workings, they foolishly trusted the industry to provide reliable, honest service and products. While millions were spent on security to prevent unauthorized access to the physical structures that housed these organizations and governments, they had left their back door open, unlocked and unprotected. No one would ever suspect this type of crime. By following ABM's setup instructions, they would be leaving themselves vulnerable.

No wonder ABM had made such dramatic financial gains over the last several months. It was becoming clear to James that these gains had been accomplished by illicit means and not great financial, or intellectual business prowess. ABM had taken the easy route. The company had access to inside information from almost all of the major institutions, even political leaders, who were using their newest ABM computers. The list of names was impressive. In fact, James now surmised that the two files were only a partial list of those names. Monika had somehow stumbled upon a major conspiracy. She would be in the greatest danger. ABM would not let any individual expose them. They were in a position of wealth and power, and would not permit their continued existence to be threatened. They would have amassed tremendous amounts of personal political information that could be used to protect their own interests as well as making them a financial monster. They could black mail any politician or agency who threatened them by using the private data they had collected. ABM would be an ominous foe. There was no knowing how far their tentacles reached.

The ramifications of this scheme staggered James. Now that he had unencrypted the files, he felt an urgency to talk to Monika. He needed to reassure himself that she was safe. He needed to warn her to be careful. He wished that he had gone with her and not remained behind. Perhaps if he had gone with her none of this would have happened. He would never forgive himself if anything happened to her.

Monika's imminent danger made James forget the argument they had had before she took off. He realized how much he loved her and wanted her. He had been a fool to let her go. All that mattered to him now was her safety. Nothing else held any significance. Without her, there would be little meaning to his life.

James was surprised by the strength of his feelings. They were just as powerful as in San Francisco, when he had believed that he had lost her to the icy waters of the Bay. He wondered how he had allowed his awareness of his need for Monika to become dimmed over the past year. Why had he allowed his work to take up so much of his time and emotion? He had become distant with her. He now realized his mistakes. Mistakes that might have already taken her from him. He began to panic. He picked up the phone and punched in directory assistance. The operator answered.

"What city?"

"Toronto, Canada."

"Go ahead."

"The Harbor Weston Hotel."

There was a pause and then an automated voice gave the number and offered to connect for a fifty cent charge, if the pound key was pressed. James pressed the pound symbol on his phone keypad. He could hear the number being dialed. The phone rang at the other end.

"Weston Harbor Hotel." It was a man's voice.

"Monika Queller please." James checked the time. There was a three hour difference. It would be early afternoon there. He hoped Monika was in her room.

"That's room 1711 South. I'll connect you." The hotel clerk was polite and made the connection. Monika's room phone rang.

"Come on. Be there," James encouraged.

After several rings the hotel operator came back on the line.

"Sorry sir." This time it was a female who spoke. "There's no answer. May I take a message?"

James thought, then answered, "No. Thank you," and hung up the phone. He felt his heart drop. Maybe it was too late?

James got up from his desk. He felt a cold heavy feeling looming inside his person. He felt sick. He had to inform his superiors immediately about this discovery. There was no hiding the fact that ABM was involved in some questionable behavior and that it warranted closer scrutiny. More importantly, he had to get to Toronto and help Monika. If he was right, and she had stumbled upon this information innocently, then she was in great jeopardy.

●

James arrived at LAX just in time to catch the noon flight to Toronto. It had not taken long for him to explain the situation to his superiors. They had been surprised by his allegations at first, but when he had brought them to his office and gone over the data contained in the files that Monika had sent him, slowly it became evident to them that there was something going on.

ABM had made some interesting investments over the past few months in places in the world that most considered too risky to do business. In every venture that ABM had chosen, the company seemed to have had a knack of winning out against all commonly held advice. This had been brought to the attention of the CIA, who had been doing a very light routine review of ABM without their knowledge; even James had not been aware of this investigation. When he approached his superiors, they were intrigued by the coincidence of the files surfacing.

It was decided to send James to Toronto to investigate, but not alone. They would notify the proper Canadian agencies and ask for their assistance. Since it was their L.A. office that had stumbled upon this information first, they felt a joint operation with the Canadians was warranted. This type of cooperation was not unusual between the two countries. James would be met by them in Toronto that evening at the airport. He was to work closely with his Canadian counterparts and was placed under strict orders not to cause any international embarrassment.

James had not packed. He had immediately driven to the airport. He would pick things up as he required them at the other end. At LAX he had put his car into the 'Park and Fly' service and hurried to the American ticket agent.

Being a Monday, the flight was not very booked. James easily bought a ticket. He did not have his passport with him; it was not necessary for travel into Canada. All he needed was his driver's license to prove his identity to Canadian immigration. Since he was being met at the other end, he did not anticipate any difficulties.

He went right to the gate and boarded the plane. He was anxious about Monika. He sat in his seat and fastened his seat belt. He hoped that he would not be too late. He prayed that she was safe. He could not bear to think of a life without her.

Chapter 9

D own the stairs Monika scrambled. Her purse was flopping around so much she looped its strap over her head and across her chest. The CDs were inside and she needed them. This way she would not lose the purse or the CDs.

The man pursuing her was gradually gaining on her. She tried to quicken her pace. As she descended, she began to remove her shoes one by one without stopping. As she removed each one, she held on to it, one in each hand. She grabbed onto the handrail that went along the center of the stairwell. This way she could now go faster down the stairs. It was her only hope. Her pursuer would catch up with her if she kept going at the slower speed that wearing the shoes forced her to travel.

Monika was getting closer to the end of the stairwell. On every new level there was a sign posted upon the door that led to that floor indicating its number. She was encouraged to now be at the third floor. The next level was the mezzanine. She recalled the floor setup from the buttons in the elevator. The first floor was the main lobby, the next the mezzanine, followed by the third floor.

She tried to look up the stairwell without stopping to gauge the progress of her pursuer. It was difficult to concentrate on her escape forward while turning her head back and looking up. She could not easily see anything, but from the sound of the footsteps, he was very close. Monika assumed it was a man by the loud sound of the footsteps echoing in the stairwell. Men were much heavier on their feet. From the sounds, she determined that it was only one man chasing after her.

As she neared the mezzanine exit, she worried that there may be someone else there awaiting her. Perhaps an associate of the man above, who might try to stop her. She realized that there was no sense thinking about that possibility. There was nothing that she could do about it now. She would deal with the situation if it arose, but hoped that it wouldn't.

Monika was getting tired as she continued her non-stop descent. It was good that she kept herself in shape. Hopefully she would be in better condition than the man above, and be able to outlast him.

When she came to the mezzanine exit from the stairs, she slowed her pace, put on her shoes as she hurried along, opened the door that led to the mezzanine from the stairwell, and took a very quick reconnoiter. The mezzanine had one or two people in it. It was not busy. There appeared to be no other threat. Monika walked out into the mezzanine and tried to compose herself as she walked quickly to a large curving stairway. From a sign hanging from the ceiling above her, she discovered that the stairway led down to the west side of the main lobby.

She crossed the mezzanine to the stairs and started down. She took one quick look to the stairwell door. She saw that her pursuer had not caught up to her. He had not yet exited from the stairwell to the mezzanine.

Down she went, trying not to be too conspicuous. When she arrived at the lobby at the base of the stairs, she looked around. There were many people in the area. She felt very nervous not knowing if one of these people might be connected with her pursuer. She could not go back to her room, nor did she feel that she should exit the hotel through the lobby and the front entrance.

She paused and again looked around.

On the wall across from her there was another sign. The sign indicated that the stairs from the lobby led to a floor below, to an exit for the ferry. That was it. The ferry. She recalled reading in the tourist information about the hotel, that had been sent to her by the festival organizers, that a ferry dock was right at the foot of the Harbor Weston. The ferry crossed from the hotel city side to the islands every twenty minutes. If she could get to the ferry and was lucky enough to catch one, she might be able to get away.

●

The man in the stairwell was only a couple of floors behind and above Monika. He had heard the noise of a door opening and closing. The clatter of Monika's footsteps stopped after the sound of the closing door. He realized that she must have exited. He increased his speed. He was almost upon her. He did not want to have to tell Kazinski that Ms. Queller had gotten away and that he had failed to get her or the CDs.

He tore down the remaining stairs 'til he came to the mezzanine exit. Opening the door he hurried out of the stairwell and into the mezzanine. His entry had been so abrupt that the few people who were standing around the area were drawn to investigate what had caused such a loud disturbance to their calm afternoon. The man paid no attention to them. His only concern was finding his prey.

Quickly scanning the room, the man noted that the only means of escape was down a set of wide curved stairs on the southwest wall of the mezzanine. He ran across to them and continued his pursuit. He sensed that he was very close to catching Monika.

There was no one else on the stairs as he came to the lobby below. He stopped to visually scan the lobby for any sign of her. The area seemed calm and undisturbed. It did not seem that anything untoward had happened here in the last few minutes.

The man noted that the stairs went down one more floor. He saw the same sign that Monika had read just a moment before: 'Ferry'. Yes. He was sure that this would be her only choice. She was trying to get to the ferry. That was what he would do in the circumstances.

He crossed to the stairs and began to move down them in haste.

●

On the floor below, Monika found herself amongst several boutiques that rented premises from the hotel. The shops were situated along a long hallway that led to two full-size glass doors and eventually outside. She could see a pathway and people passing by outside. There was a sign on the wall opposite her indicating that the ferry was through these doors. She was tired but there was no stopping now.

The hallway was empty and dark compared to the crowd and brightness of the outside sunlight. That light was shining into the hallway through the glass doors. Monika made for the doors. There was no sign of her pursuer on the stairs behind her, but that did not reassure her. He might appear at any moment. She would not feel safe until she had made it onto the ferry and gotten away from here. She was feeling afraid and tired. She also felt a little light-headed from hunger. She had only had a light breakfast. All this exertion had placed a strenuous demand upon her system.

●

The man found his way down to the lower level and the boutiques. He was out of breath but not exhausted from the chase. He did not waste time searching the area, but quickly headed for the door that led to the outside and the ferry docks. He knew where she was going. He could catch up. He opened the doors and went out into the sunlight. It took a few seconds for him to adjust to the sudden bright light. He brought up his right hand to act as a sun visor to aid him in his search.

●

Upon going outside, Monika had been blinded by the light. In her panic, she did not want to waste time waiting to get her bearings. She squinted as she looked for the ferry docks. The exit from the hotel was at the street level.

Monika found herself on a path that went along the perimeter of the harborfront. To the north the path led along the west side of the hotel to the main street of the harborfront. Directly west and opposite from the hotel was a high-rise that looked like a condominium residence. There was a causeway at the mezzanine level that linked the condominium like an umbilical cord to the hotel. Both buildings seemed to have been designed and built by the same contractor. In-between the hotel and condominium was a large knoll of beautifully manicured grass. To the south about fifty feet was the harbor and the islands beyond.

Immediately to the southeast was a one story cement facade which had a large sign attached to it: 'Toronto Island Ferry'. There was a small line-up of people buying tickets.

All of this took only seconds for Monika to take in as she stood outside the hotel in open view. The loud blowing of a ship's horn went off. The sudden noise startled her back to reality and the urgency of her purpose. It was the first warning from the currently docked ferry boat of its impending departure. She began to run toward the ticket booth. She needed to catch that ferry.

She quickly ran the fifty feet to the ticket booth. There were only two people in front of her. She saw the fare sign above the ticket booth and opened her purse to get out the required amount of money. She was very fidgety as she waited in line. She was beginning to mutter out loud, 'Hurry up.'

●

Once his eyes had adjusted, the man could clearly see the surrounding area and the ferry docks about fifty feet away. He saw the ticket booth and a young woman buying a ticket. The woman turned around. He saw the fear in her body language even from this distance. It was her. He started to run toward the ferry docks.

●

Monika was growing impatient. The ferry docks was an area that lay behind the ticket booth. There was no way to get access other than by passing through the ticket booth gate. Once past the ticket booth, there was a barred-in waiting area much like a prison courtyard.

The bars went around the perimeter of the ferry docks. There were a series of sliding gates that led to the boats. Two ferry boats were docked. One of the gates to the boats was open and a scruffy looking employee in his light blue shirt with the logo of the city sewn to his breast pocket was standing by the gate. The passengers that had been ahead of Monika at the ticket booth were quickly hurrying over to the gate and boarding the ramp to the one ferry boat that was almost loaded. The gate man was getting ready to close the gate and send the boat on its way.

It was Monika's turn to buy her ticket.

"Hi. One please. Can I still make this one?" she asked through the circular hole that was cut in the ticket booth window.

"Yeah. You'll just make it." The employee gave Monika her ticket.

Monika turned to look behind her as she grabbed the ticket. Off in the distance next to the hotel exit was a very large man in a dark suit standing and looking around. He seemed to be out of breath as if he had just been under some sort of strenuous activity. She instantly sensed that this was her pursuer and turned her head back. She hurried ahead into the barred-in courtyard and toward the gate for the ferry boat. The gate man was beginning to slide the gate closed and the ramp to the ferry boat was being raised.

"Wait! Wait!" Monika shouted to the gate man.

The gate man looked over and, upon seeing such a pretty young woman, decided that he would wait for this last passenger.

"Hold on. One last one," he said to the men on the ferry boat that were preparing to leave.

"Hurry up," the gate man yelled over to her.

Monika made more of an effort. She came up to the gate. The gate man was smiling.

"Thank you." She was out of breath.

"No problem," the gate man replied.

She walked past the gate. The gate man slid it closed and locked it behind them. Both he and Monika were on the boat side of the bars. She walked onto the ramp to the ferry boat and into safety.

⬤

Monika's pursuer realized what was happening. When he got to the ticket booth, he ran right through, ignoring the call of the ticket booth employee.

"Hey. You need a ticket."

The man ran up to the gate and grabbed onto the bars.

"Hey. You. Open the gate," he called to the gate man who was on the other side.

"Too late," was all that he said. The gate man walked away and ignored the man.

There was no point in arguing. There was no way to get past the locked gate and onto the ferry. The ferry was now starting to pull away from the dock. The man hit the bars and tugged at them in his frustration at missing the boat and coming so close to capturing Monika. He watched helplessly as the boat made its way out of the docks and into the harbor.

⬤

Monika was relieved that she had made it onto the boat. The ferry boat was reminiscent of old Mississippi riverboats. It had a main deck that was made of a highly-polished wood. The deck was enclosed and protected from the elements. There was a series of windows along the entire length of both sides of the deck that gave a

panoramic view of the harbor and islands. Monika walked into the protected area and carefully viewed through the windows the dock behind. She saw the man who had been chasing her standing at the closed gate. He was obviously angry and frustrated at not getting onto the ferry. Monika smiled. She was safe for the moment. She got a good look at the man and then moved away and deeper into the boat. She made her way to the other end of the boat through the crowd that was standing inside the covered deck. Both ends of the boat were the same in design and layout. The boat could go in either direction without needing to turn around. It was a very utilitarian design. There was a wide stairway in front of this end's ramp as there was at the other end where she had entered onto the ferry. The stairs were also made of wood and led up about ten feet to another deck. She decided to go up.

The second deck was open to the light breeze of the lake. Above it was a ceiling filled with orange life jackets. There was another deck above. It was on this uppermost third level that the ship's captain navigated the boat from his commanding view of the harbor and lake.

Monika walked over to the balustrade and railing that enclosed the side of the boat, on this second open deck. Leaning against the rail she drew in the refreshing lake air. The ferry boat was well into the harbor. The docks were becoming a speck along the shore.

She admired the skyline with its skyscrapers on the east, the tower and a domed structure that looked like a stadium on the west. She felt at ease. She looked at her wristwatch. It was 12:40 PM. She wondered what she would do about Andrew's call at two. She wondered if it would be safe to go back to the hotel, at least until she managed to get in touch with him. The thought occurred to her that the man at the dock might wait at the docks for her to return. She was unsure of her next move. She wondered if there was anyone here that could help her, but she realized that that was not possible. Kazinski was far too powerful in this city and she would only find herself in a more precarious situation. The best plan was to connect with Andrew and then see what they could do next. It was obvious to her that Kazinski was a very dangerous and powerful man.

Monika remained at the railing as the ferry cut through the water. It was a short ride across the harbor and would probably take only fifteen minutes. She decided to rest until the boat docked at the island. Once there, she could find out if there was any other way off the island and back to the city side than via the ferry docks at the foot of the hotel. She would ask one of the crew on the ferry after it docked.

She gazed out into the harbor. There was an airplane passing overhead making its approach.

Monika watched as it passed over the ferry boat and came lower to the water. On the other side of the harbor, on the western-most part of the island, there was a small airport. That part of the island was very close to the mainland. Maybe she could find a way through there to get back to the hotel. The distance from the airport along the harbor-front to the hotel was not more than a mile or so.

●

At the ferry docks, the man had turned away from the gate and gone back to the ticket booth. He leaned down to speak to the attendant.

"When's the next ferry?"

"Twenty minutes."

"Thanks."

He walked back through the ticket booth area towards the hotel. There was no point going after her. He knew the islands well. There was no knowing if she would return via the ferry docks or go through the airport ferry. The best thing was to go back to his partner and phone Kazinski. He did not like the idea of having to report to his boss without the CDs or the girl. Kazinski had a foul temper when he was angered. There was no telling what might happen. Still, there was nothing that he could do to avoid it. The girl had been quicker than he had expected. If it had not been for the incredible bad luck of missing the ferry, he would have her now.

The man made his way back along the path to

the hotel. He entered the building and found his way back up to the lobby and his partner, who was still waiting in the car in the driveway. He crossed through the revolving door and up to the car. He opened the door and got in.

"What kept you? Where is she?" his partner asked, not knowing what had transpired.

"I lost her."

"What?"

"I went up to her room and she took off. I chased her, but she managed to get on the ferry before I could stop her."

"We'd better let Kazinski know right away." His partner picked up the car phone and dialed.

●

In his office Kazinski was alone. He was going through the files in his desk to see if anything else had been disturbed or taken. He was mad that Monika had been able to fool him. It would not happen again. He vowed to get even with her for this blow to his ego.

The phone rang. Kazinski saw his private line button light up. He picked up the receiver.

"Yes."

The partner handed the phone over to the man. He was not the one who lost Monika so he wasn't going to be the one to report.

"Sir. We've lost her."

There was a long pause at the other end as Kazinski controlled his anger.

"She got away on the ferry."

"And the CDs?" Kazinski now spoke in a controlled manner.

"She probably has them on her."

Kazinski was furious. He wondered if Monika understood the importance of the CDs. He considered what his next move should be before he spoke. If those CDs got into the wrong hands both he and ABM would be screwed.

"There's something else." The man did not wait for Kazinski to respond.

"I think there is someone else involved. She left a message at the front desk for a guy called Ambrose. Andrew Ambrose. I pretended to be him and got the message." The man stopped and awaited Kazinski's reaction to this additional bit of news.

Kazinski was taken aback. He knew the name, but Ambrose was dead … unless. It must be his son. The son was digging into his father's death. It was a complication that Kazinski had not foreseen.

"Find out where this Andrew Ambrose is and bring him to the old warehouse. Don't mess this up. I want him alive and I want it done quietly."

"Yes sir."

"Call me here when you've got him."

"Yes sir." The man hung up the phone.

Kazinski was less agitated. He now had something to bargain with. He would trade the CDs for

Ambrose. Once he got the CDs he would dispose of both Ambrose and Monika.

●

The trip across the lake had helped. Monika was now more calm. It was a wonderfully warm and sunny day. After the boat had tied up, she went down to the main deck and asked one of the crew, who was standing to one side, for directions.

"Excuse me," Monika asked.

"Yeah?"

The crew member was curt, but pleased to talk with a pretty woman. He had long hair and wore the dirty blue uniform of the employees of the ferry service. Monika couldn't help but think what a terrible impression of the city these employees gave. She was amazed that there was not a higher standard required or enforced.

"Is there any way back to the city other than through here?" she continued.

"Yeah. You can go by Hanlan's or the airport."

"Do they both go back to the ferry dock?"

"Not the airport ferry. It crosses the western gap and lands near Spadina."

"How do I get to the airport ferry?"

"You can't. It's only for the airport. There's no access to the rest of the island. You'd have to cross the runway." The crewman was becoming more friendly.

"Oh." Monika's heart dropped.

Seeing her disappointment, the crewman added:

"Or you can take a water taxi."

"Water taxi?" Monika had never known that there were such things.

"Yeah. It's about ten bucks."

"Where can I get the taxi?" Monika's spirits lifted. This was the way to get safely back to the city without using the ferry.

"Over there."

The crewman was becoming curt again as it became clear to him that this woman was only interested in information. He pointed over to the other side of the island dock to a small building that was next to a large terraced restaurant overlooking the harbor and city.

"Thanks." Monika turned and walked down the ramp, onto the solid land of the island.

The island was kept by the city as a park. It did not allow any vehicles other than the ones used by the groundskeepers. There was a series of three major islands that contained: three yacht clubs, a couple of restaurants, vast areas of open space, public beaches and a small amusement park. These islands were all linked together and over the years had been greatly altered and added to by man. They stretched about two miles across the main downtown section of the city from their position in the lake. Their busiest time of use was now, during the summer. Since it was a weekday the island was not that busy. It was a good time for sightseeing, but Monika did not have the time.

She had to get back to the city side as fast as she could. Andrew would be calling and she did not want to miss his call. She resolved herself to the fact that she somehow had to sneak back into her room. She had to connect with Andrew and it was the only way possible to do it. She had no other means of communicating with him, and she needed to speak with him. She would be careful but she had to return to the hotel at least until she heard from him.

With renewed determination, Monika started along the path to where the ferry crewman had directed her. The path skirted along the docking area over to a small protected inlet. The water in the inlet was out of the main force of the lake and sheltered from the wake of the ferries. She came up to a small shack-like structure. There was a hand painted sign that had seen better days: Water Taxi. There was no one in the shack. There was a small landing. Secured to it was a small boat.

The boat was dirty white in color. There was a small cabin area which was open to the elements. It contained a windshield with a small covering overhead to protect the driver, steering wheel, chrome throttle and a bench seat. The throttle was the only shiny object in the boat, polished from its constant use. It was very spartan. There was a salty-looking man, with a three-days growth of a white-ish grey beard, lying on the bench seat of the open cockpit area, asleep. He had a grimy old

New York Yankees baseball cap pulled low on his head. He was in his late fifties and very unkempt. He reminded Monika of an old Papa Hemingway type. She walked onto the landing and tried to get his attention.

"Ahem." She cleared her throat so as to awaken the man. He did not stir.

"Ahem." She was louder. She scrutinized him, but there had been no effect.

"Ahem." She tried again, but even louder. Still there was no change. Monika turned away in frustration.

"What do you want?" came matter-of-factly from the man. There was no change in his position or body. Only the voice which had emanated from him was testament to his being alive.

Monika was startled. She turned back to examine the old man. Seeing no change in him, she wondered if she had imagined the voice. She stepped cautiously closer on the landing.

"Hello? Did you say something?" she inquired of the still motionless man. She kept approaching.

"What do you want?" the man clearly spoke but remained still.

"Is this the water taxi?" Monika had not imagined the voice and was now curious to identify the man.

"Yeah lady," was all that he said.

"Well are you working today? Can I get a ride?" She was sarcastic and becoming aggressive towards him.

With that said, and the tone understood, the man lifted his baseball cap and stared into her eyes. There was a mischievous glint in them.

"Yeah. Come on aboard." He smiled and got up from his reclining position.

Monika was proud of herself and thought he was getting up to help her. Instead, the man bypassed her and got out of the boat to untie the lines. Monika was stunned and stood glaring at him.

"Well do you want a ride or not?" the taxi man asked sarcastically.

"Whew." Monika made an angry expression under her breath and stepped down from the landing into the boat.

The taxi driver chuckled and ignored her. He threw the lines into the boat and then hopped on board. He grabbed onto the steering wheel and turned a key on the right side next to the chrome throttle. The boat made a low groaning sound and then started up. Monika sat down at the stern of the boat. A large black cloud billowed out of the exhaust behind her. The exhaust wafted into the boat before dissipating. Monika waved her hands and coughed.

"Oh. Sorry." The taxi driver turned to see. He had a slight grin on his face. "So where are we going?"

"To the city." Monika was displeased but there

was no point getting upset. It was only a short ride and she needed to get to the city as soon as possible.

"Whereabouts?"

Monika thought a moment. She had not realized that the taxi would drop her anywhere. "Close to the Weston Hotel but not near the ferry docks."

"Okay. How about the Terminal building?" the man suggested.

"Where's that?"

The man turned and pointed across the harbor. "There. That green building there. It's about a five minute walk to the Weston."

Monika followed his pointing finger and could see the place he meant. It was right next to the building where she had given her reading on Sunday. She knew where it was.

"Yes. That would be great."

"That'll be ten bucks." The driver waited for Monika's acceptance.

"Yes. Sure."

The driver pulled down on the steering wheel and slowly pushed the throttle down. The boat moved away from the landing and gradually picked up speed. They cleared the docking area and into the open water.

The sound of the taxi's motor was loud. There was no way to talk and be heard over the noise. Not that the conversation would be of much interest between her and the driver. She sat quietly in the stern and fell into thought. She had only been here in Emerald City three days, yet so much had happened that it felt longer. She wondered how it would all end. She had never considered that she would be in this type of predicament. She thought of James.

'Maybe if he had come I wouldn't have gotten involved in all this,' she thought.

She hoped that James had gotten the e-mail. She did not feel as alone knowing that he would receive her note. After she spoke with Andrew, she was going to call James. She missed him and wanted to hear his voice. She wanted to know that he still cared; she wanted him to know that she was sorry to have left him that way. Finding herself in this situation had made her forget the reason for the argument they had had. She realized even more that she loved him; she wanted to try and work things out. The trip here could have been so different if she had not come alone. It could have been such a lovely time to have shared together.

The water taxi was well under way. It would not be long before it arrived on the city side. Until then she was safe from harm on the water. This trip provided her a special opportunity—a time to settle herself. She tried to strengthen her resolve to see everything through and to help Andrew, but privately she feared what might lie ahead. It might be a long time before she was this safe again. The loud drone of the motor cut her off from all other concerns of the real world. She relaxed herself and reveled in these few moments of safety. The breeze, created as the boat sped through the gently undulating water, caressed her. She felt her skin tighten with a sudden surge of goose bumps.

●

Andrew worked at a marketing company not far from the waterfront. It did not take very long for Kazinski's two men to find out where he was. They made only four calls before they had all the information on him: where he lived and worked. The company he worked for was nearby on King Street, west of the Chinatown area. Kazinski's men had called and checked with the receptionist to see if he was at work. When they were informed that he was in the office only 'til one thirty and then would be out for the rest of the day, they hurriedly drove from the Weston Hotel to his place of work.

They arrived and parked right in front of the old building that housed Andrew's office. It was right next to a popular strip joint in a seedy section of town. The two men got out of their car and entered the structure.

The building was not well kept. Though there was a fresh coat of an insipid blue paint on the outside walls, it was still dilapidated looking. Kazinski's men entered the building. They found the directory for the building on the right wall as they entered. It was inside a yellowing display next to the elevator. They checked through it. The marketing company was on the fourth and top floor.

The men pressed for the elevator which very slowly responded. Soon a circular light above the door lit up to indicate its arrival. The door did not open, but the light stayed on. There was a tiny window in the elevator outside door through which the men peered, to see what was causing the delay.

It was an old style elevator that required the outer door to be opened manually. Understanding the problem, one of the men pulled at a lever on the outer door and slid it open. Inside, the actual elevator was waiting. Both men got into the tiny space and manually closed the door. One of them pushed the button for the fourth floor. The elevator strained on its way upward with the weight of the two large men.

It was a rickety ride. Each upper elevator door they passed had the same tiny window through which they could see the next floor. It was a slow journey. When the elevator finally arrived at the fourth floor it stopped with a jerking motion before coming to a complete halt. One of the men leaned forward and pulled on the inside lever of the door and opened it. They both stepped out onto the landing that creaked under their weight as they walked. They came to an opaque glass paneled wood door. Upon the door in black lettering was the name of the company.

They opened the door and walked into a reception area. There was a reception desk and a young woman, wearing a hands-free phone headset, sitting behind the desk. The two men walked up to the desk.

"Can I help you gentlemen?" the receptionist inquired.

"Mr. Ambrose please." The man who had chased after Monika did all the talking. He spoke in a very official way.

"Is he expecting you?"

"No."

He leaned over the desk and brought out a small leather wallet. He flashed a police detective's badge at her, and as he continued, put it away.

"It's kind of a delicate matter." He smiled as he spoke in a quieter voice so as not to be overheard by anyone else.

The receptionist seemed to comprehend and did not question further. "I'll ring through for him. Do you want to take a seat?"

"Thank you." The man stood back up and with his partner stepped over to a leather sofa and sat down. They both listened as the receptionist rang through for Andrew.

"Andrew? There's two gentlemen here to see you. Should I send them in?" She fell silent and listened to the response. "Okay."

She pushed a button and disconnected from Andrew. She looked over to the man who had spoken to her.

"He'll be right out."

"Thank you," the man said.

"Can I get you a coffee?"

"No. We're fine. Thanks."

"Okay." The receptionist, having done her duty, returned to her phone.

The two men waited patiently. After a few minutes Andrew came through a door to the right of the reception area and made eye contact with the two men as they looked up.

"Hi. I'm Andrew Ambrose. How can I help you?" He walked over to them as they stood up and offered each of them his hand.

"Mr. Andrew Ambrose?" the same man spoke. "I'm Detective Mackee, and this is Detective Burns." Both men rapidly took out and flashed their badges, and just as rapidly put them away, under the guise of trying not to embarrass him.

"What's the problem?" Andrew asked cautiously. This situation reminded him of the way in which he had been informed of his father's murder. It brought back all those awful memories to him.

"No problem. We are investigating your father's..." he became delicate, "...case. We think we've stumbled upon something and won-

dered if you could come with us to the station?"

"Like what?" Andrew was relieved that it wasn't bad news and elated that the police were obviously taking a second look at the case after all his requests.

"We'd rather not discuss it here, if you understand? We'd like to show you some things at the station…that we have come across."

"When?"

"Now would be best. It won't take long. We could have you back here within the hour."

Andrew checked the time on his watch. "Well it is lunch time. I 'spose I could come now, but I have an important call to make at two."

"That's not a problem. We should be back by then but, if not, you can use a phone at the station." The man offered a quick solution.

"Well, I'd rather just come back here to make the call. Just in case I need some information from my files." Andrew pretended it was a business call. He did not want to call Monika from the police station and take a chance of having his plan to search through Kazinski's office files overheard.

"No problem. We'll get you back," the man assured Andrew.

"Okay. Let's go," Andrew accepted. He turned to speak to the receptionist. "Marlee. I'm out for lunch. I'll be back at two."

"Okay Mr. Ambrose."

Chapter 10

The water taxi cruised in-between the Terminal building on its left and a large condominium building on its right. Both buildings jutted out into the harbor on land that created two peninsulas that only they occupied, allowing the lake to fill the two hundred foot space between them. On the Terminal side, several large cruise ships were moored. The sight of them from the taxi was impressive. The water inside this jetty was much more calm than the open harbor.

On the land between the buildings, ahead, about one hundred feet, was a smaller structure that looked like an old two-car garage. This building had been refurbished. It was a little coffee shop which had an outside patio for its customers, facing the harbor. There were several black metal tables and chairs. A few people were seated and enjoying their coffee and the view out to the lake from this very pretty setting.

Behind the coffee shop was the main roadway of the harborfront. Beyond the roadway, the skyscrapers of Emerald City suddenly loomed.

The taxi cruised to a dock just to the left of the coffee shop on the Terminal side and pulled up to the dock. Without stopping its engine, the driver indicated to Monika that she should climb out onto the dock.

"Here you are."

"Thanks." Monika handed the driver his ten dollar fare.

"Anytime," was all that the driver said.

Monika stepped out of the taxi and onto the solid ground of city side. The taxi revved up its engines and pulled away.

Monika stood for a moment trying to get her bearings. She felt very claustrophobic amongst these tall buildings after having experienced the openness of the island and lake. She checked the time on the clock of the Terminal building that was high above her: 1:16. She walked out from the dock onto the cement sidewalk and the road.

It was an interesting road. It was very wide and had two lanes going in each direction, which is what Monika expected to see. What she didn't expect were the two tracks running along a slight-ly raised central median which separated the east from west roadway. A quaint red streetcar rang its bell as it drove past going west. Monika was pleasantly surprised to see such a sight. She took a look up and down the road as the street car went by.

There was a sign post reading 'Queen's Quay West' at an intersection just in front of the coffee shop. The road that abutted Queen's Quay was York Street. About a hundred yards farther up towards the city was a circular 'on ramp' that led right to the raised expressway that she had trav-eled upon when she came from the airport. The expressway seemed to be the demarcation between the main downtown city core and the waterfront. It was quite a contrast.

Looking west Monika could see that Queen's Quay went on for at least two miles. There were several highrises lining it on both sides. The most outstanding of these buildings were the CN Tower and the domed structure that she had first viewed from the water taxi in the harbor. It was obvious-ly a stadium of some sort. Monika did not know the name of the stadium. She did not pay much attention to sporting events or their facilities. She leaned her head back for a moment to better see to the top of the tower. She felt a little vertigo from looking up at the overpowering tower so she dropped her view back to ground level.

Looking east there was a parking lot on the north side of the road, and then a newly built office complex. Further along there was another intersection with a road running north. This road was about two hundred yards east of her present position. Just beyond the intersection, at the second story level, was a covered walkway that spanned Queen's Quay from a tall building on the south side to another on the north. This was the Weston Hotel. She could see the large white lettering of the hotel's logo and name affixed to the building at the level of the walkway. The building it joined on the north side had a large sign on it at the same level as the hotel's logo. It was a convention complex that belonged to the Weston. The hotel buildings were about a city block away.

Bringing her view back along the south side of the road, she saw that there were three skyscrapers and then the coffee shop. It would be no more than a five minute walk.

There was plenty of time to get to the hotel and find a way back to her room. She wondered if Kazinski's man would be there waiting for her, or maybe there was more than one. She would be stupid to just walk right in through either the main lobby or dockside entrance. Perhaps there was another way. She had to get back to her room for Andrew's call. It was the only thing she could think to do. She hoped that Andrew would have some ideas. In any event she would feel safer knowing there was someone else here in this city involved with her in this predicament. But what if Andrew didn't call; or what if she was captured by Kazinski's men? She had to get rid of the CDs before she got to her room. But how?

Monika started to walk along the sidewalk towards the hotel as she pondered her next move. She crossed in front of the coffee shop and considered buying a drink, but changed her mind. She was becoming nervous about what fate might meet her at the hotel. She kept going. In the next building she saw a convenience store. Suddenly an idea struck her. She walked over to the convenience store and went inside.

The convenience store was brightly lit. Monika went down the aisles 'til she came to the stationery section. She was looking for an envelope that she could put the CDs into. She came to the section and found an envelope of the correct size. She had a plan. She took the envelope and went to the counter to pay. At the counter there was some coffee and pastries.

"That all?" a Chinese woman said to her in broken English.

"No. Give me a coffee and one of those." Monika indicated a decadent-looking pastry. This would keep her going until she could get a real meal.

The woman grabbed the pastry with a piece of tissue.

"Don't put it in a bag. I'll take it like that." Monika directed.

"You help self coffee." She showed Monika the paper cups and rang up the total in her cash register. "Four thirty seven." The woman announced what was owed.

Monika opened her purse and found a Canadian five dollar bill. It was blue and reminded her of play money. She handed it to the woman who took it and gave her change.

"Thank you." Monika put the change back in her purse and moved to one side to pour her coffee.

Taking her coffee and envelope, Monika left the store. Outside she found a raised cement tree planter and sat down on its ledge. She placed the coffee and pastry on the ledge and opened her purse. She took out a pen and wrote her name and room number upon the envelope. She then carefully, and in as concealed a way as possible, slipped the two CDs into the envelope and sealed it. She put the envelope into her purse, along with the pen, and closed it. That accomplished, she picked up her coffee and pastry. She took a couple of minutes to eat and enjoy the drink, keeping her eye out for anything or anybody that might be suspicious.

As she drank the coffee she regarded the hotel. It was not far away. She wondered how she could get in without being seen. She considered the walkway which crossed from the hotel's convention center into what appeared to be its mezzanine level—but there might be someone there waiting for her. She decided to walk by the hotel and see what she could see before making her decision.

Getting up from the planter, now that she had finished her snack, she continued along the sidewalk to the hotel. The sidewalk was very busy with people coming and going. She was not worried about being seen. There were too many people for her to be easily observed; she was hidden amongst them.

As she approached the intersection at the hotel, a large crowd was coming out from the ferry docks. The ferry must have just come in and let off its passengers. There were a couple of hot dog vendors and an ice cream truck parked nearby, which added to the congestion. Monika crossed through the crowd and continued to walk along the sidewalk that crossed along the front of the hotel.

The entrance to the hotel was hidden from view from the sidewalk by a terraced garden wall that was all part of the hotel building. She could see that several taxi cabs were parked along the driveway that rose up inside. Monika kept walking. She was very nervous. She walked in front of the hotel, passed its driveway entrance and came to a side street that ran along the hotel's grey cement eastern-most wall, which separated the hotel building from a harbor jetty and a boat cruise operation. Several of its small boats were moored along the side street in the harbor. Monika stopped and looked down the side street.

At the end of the street was a gated area which had a large sign across the top of its twelve foot high gate: NO ENTRY TO FERRY. DO NOT ENTER. The gate was at the end of the side street about one hundred and fifty feet away. A ferry boat could be seen docked there on the other side in the harbor.

Halfway along the side street there was a large opening in the hotel's wall out of which stuck the front portion of a large delivery truck. It was the hotel delivery and loading bay. The side street was narrow and it was a wonder that the truck had been able to maneuver its way into that position. Monika made her decision. She could find her way back into the hotel through the loading bay. She did not expect that Kazinski's men would be there waiting for her.

Monika hurried down the side street. There were cars parallel parked along the hotel side of the street. There was not one person on the street. She came up to the truck and carefully crossed in front of it and then slipped into the loading area.

The loading bay entrance was cool from the air conditioning of the hotel. The area was dark. There was a short stairway ahead that led to a glass window and a closed doorway. Monika hurried over to the stairs, keeping an eye out for somebody. She climbed up the stairs and peered into the glass window.

Behind the window was a little office. This was obviously a security office that kept track of those coming and going through this entrance. No one was there. Monika did not waste time but opened the door which, to her surprise, was not locked, and crept past the security office into a long brightly-lit corridor. Everyone must be on some sort of break, she thought to herself as she made her way along the corridor.

The corridor was very narrow and weaved left and right quite a distance before reaching a set of double doors. Monika carefully opened the doors and continued on. Beyond the doors was another corridor and a set of stairs. There was a sign post on the wall indicating housekeeping straight ahead and kitchen up the stairs. Monika decided to go up.

Stealthily, Monika went up the stairs and soon found herself in front of another set of doors. She opened them and found herself amidst the noise of the preparation room of the kitchen. There were pots and pans all over. Several men dressed in the white uniform of kitchen staff were busy preparing the day's menu. No one said anything to her as she walked through the area.

On the other side of the room was another set of doors. Monika went through them and into a small alcove that contained a set of elevator doors and another set of double doors. A sign on the wall indicated that the main kitchen was through the doors and that the elevator doors in front of her were those of the service elevator to the south tower. Monika felt relieved now that she knew where she was and had found a way out of her dilemma. She would go up into the hotel through the service elevator to her floor. It would be safe and no one would see her, at least none of Kazinski's men. There was a call button to the right of the elevator door. Monika pressed it and waited. She would be happy to get out of here and back into her room.

Once the elevator arrived Monika got in and pressed seventeen. She looked at her wristwatch. It was 1:45. It was going to be close, but she should be back in her room on time for Andrew's call. This elevator was not as plush as the ones for the regular hotel patrons. It had a protective blanket against its inside walls and a dirty white light in its ceiling next to a fan that made a squeaking sound as it turned. There was a musty smell of stale perspiration. Monika grimaced at the odor.

The service elevator did not stop at any floor other than the one that had been requested by her. When it arrived at seventeen it opened into a small room. The room was about ten by ten and contained cleaning supplies as well as a house-keeping trolley. She got out of the service elevator and the door closed, leaving her alone in the room. There was a door opposite the elevator. She crossed over to it and, placing her hand upon the handle, gently opened it inward.

The door opened to reveal her floor. There was no one around. She walked into the hall and tried to figure out in which direction her room was. She saw 1716 on one of the first rooms she came to and kept going. 1715. Then 1714 and 1712. She got her key out of her purse as she came to her room, placed it in the lock and opened the door. She noticed that the door was damaged but did not stop to examine it. She hurried in, closed the door after her and leaned against it, letting out a sigh of relief. She had made it.

Putting the chain lock on the door, she went into the sitting room. Everything was the same as she had left it, except housekeeping had been in and tidied things up a bit. She went over and sat on the sofa. She checked her watch: 1:56. She was just in time.

●

Kazinski's men had gone down the elevator and were now exiting the building on King Street with Andrew. They walked over to their car. One of the men got into the driver's side and the other, with Andrew, got into the rear passenger seat. Andrew was very tiny in comparison to the overpowering size of these two hulks.

The driver started the car and pulled out into the

traffic. The other man, in the rear, sat calmly with his right hand inside his jacket. None of them said a word. Andrew was thinking about what these two officers wanted to show him at the station. Maybe he wouldn't need Monika's help after all.

The car drove east. It soon came to and passed Spadina. Andrew thought it was odd that they had not gone north on Spadina. That would have been the most direct route to the downtown police station. He did not comment, thinking that they were going to take the next north. When the car did not turn at the next road, Andrew spoke out.

"Hey. You missed the turn."

There was no response from either of the two men.

"What's going on here? I thought we were going to the downtown station." Andrew was alarmed.

"Sit still and shut up!" the man next to Andrew barked out and removed his hand from his jacket. He was holding a gun and pointing it threateningly at him as he spoke.

"What the…" Andrew panicked.

"I said shut up. Understand?"

"Who are you?" Andrew realized that there was something wrong and that these two men might not be who they presented themselves as.

"Don't try anything stupid," the man warned.

"What do you want?"

"Just shut up. You'll find out real soon." The

man kept his gun on him.

There was nothing that Andrew could do. He was trapped. He had no idea who these men really were or what they wanted. He was very afraid, though he did not outwardly show it. He fell silent and hoped that he would survive the ordeal.

The car continued traveling along King Street until it reached Yonge Street, where it turned south towards the lake. When it reached Front Street, it turned east. Fortunately for the driver, they had not hit any red lights or been forced to stop in traffic and thereby give Andrew an opportunity of escape.

The car passed the Hummingbird Center and continued east past Coffin Park and Market Square. They kept going east to Parliament then turned south. They were now in the old industrial section of the city. This area was full of abandoned buildings and older warehouses. They turned left on Mill Street and passed the old Gooderham distillery which was being converted into condominiums.

Farther along they came to Cherry Street and passed the Canari café. The café was in the middle of nowhere and was the only building that showed any signs of activity in the area. The rest of the surrounding structures were boarded up and dilapidated. Although this district was within two miles of the downtown city business center, it felt as if they were miles away and in the middle of an abandoned town.

The car continued along Mill Street and turned left. Andrew saw the street name on the corner post—Overend Street. The car drove half way up the block and pulled into the driveway of a large, boarded-up warehouse. He was feeling very uncomfortable and did not like the look of the warehouse or the reason, he suspected, that the men had brought him here.

●

The time had gone past two-thirty and there had been no call from Andrew. Monika was concerned and wondered what might have happened to him. She considered what she might do if there was no call at all. She thought about calling James, but he would be at work, wherever that was, and she did not have a number for him. Instead she decided to wait a little longer.

At 2:45 PM the phone rang. Monika sprang up from the sitting room sofa and picked up the receiver.

"Hello?" She hoped it was Andrew.

"Ms. Queller. Arthur Kazinski." There was a change in his attitude over the phone.

Monika was stunned. Why was he calling her?

"Ms. Queller, are you there?" he asked having gotten no response. He was in control and was going to play out his hand very carefully.

"Yes." Monika was not sure what she should say. She had assumed that the man who had come after her was one of Kazinski's men, but from the way he sounded on the phone, she was no longer sure if she had been correct.

"I hope I haven't disturbed you?" He was polite and gave no indication that he knew she had stolen his CDs.

"No. I was just taking a rest." She was brief and guarded in her conversation.

"I'm calling to confirm dinner."

Monika did not know what to say. She was confused. Was Kazinski not involved in sending that man after her? Had she been mistaken? If so, then who had sent him?

"Ms. Queller?" he repeated, a little irritated at her slowness to respond.

"Oh. I'm sorry…yes, of course. What time?" She went along with him, though inside she had strong doubts about it. She did not like or trust him.

"Seven. Is that alright for you?" He continued in a smooth and charming tone.

"Yes. That would be fine."

"It will give us an opportunity to chat more about your next novel. I am quite intrigued by your idea. It sounds like there could be many twists to the plot."

"Yes. I'm looking forward to it." She meant the writing of the next book.

"I'll have the car sent for you at seven then?" he confirmed.

"Yes. That would be fine."

Monika did not believe that she had agreed to have dinner with him. How stupid could she be? Yet she couldn't say no. If he was not involved then he would be disappointed by her cancellation, which might impact her relationship with her publisher. A publisher that was influenced by him. If he was involved, then it was better to find out what type of game he was playing. Until she could contact Andrew, she was caught in the middle. She had to follow through on the date, but she would protect herself. If Kazinski was behind all this, then he would want the CDs. She would not bring them with her. She would leave them in safekeeping at the front desk. She still had them in her purse in the envelope. They would be her insurance against any harm befalling her, or so she thought.

"Oh, by the way," he added as a parting word. "Do you mind if I invite someone else? I believe you know him." There was a hint of sarcasm in his voice.

Monika wondered who it might be. The only person that they both knew was Bob the publishing rep who had accompanied her to the festival. He was the only person she could think of that they both knew.

"No. Not at all." She would feel safer having someone else along with them.

"Good. I'll see you later then. I am looking forward to continuing our talk."

"Me too," Monika lied. She wanted to know who the other guest would be, but did not want to ask. Obviously Kazinski wanted her to ask, that was why he was being so vague. She sensed that something was wrong, but she did not know what it might be. She was not willing to play into his hands.

"Good-bye." Kazinski hung up.

Monika hung up the phone.

"That was odd," she wondered out loud to herself. She sat down and tried to decide what she believed about Kazinski, the CDs and the man who had chased her.

If Kazinski was not involved, which was something that she found very hard to believe seeing as her being chased started after her visit with him at his office, then who had chased her and what did they want? Why hadn't Andrew called? Was something wrong? Where was he? All of these things occurred after her meeting with Kazinski, after she had taken the CDs. She wondered what was on the CDs. If she knew that, then she could better decide about Kazinski.

If he was involved, why had he kept the dinner appointment? Why was he being so nice? Maybe he hoped she would bring the CDs and he would be able to retrieve them from her at dinner. Certainly he would not expect her to bring them with her? That would be crazy on her part. He would certainly have figured that out.

She knew the safest path to follow was not to trust him, but she was confused by the phone call. She wished Andrew would hurry up and call. She picked up the phone and punched in three digits.

"Front desk," came the reply.

"Hi. Is there anywhere I can leave my valuables for safekeeping?"

"Yes Ma'am. We can keep them in the safe at the front desk. Would you like to come down or shall I send someone up?"

Monika considered.

"Send someone up. It's 1711 South."

"Right away, Ma'am." The clerk hung up the phone.

Monika hung up the phone and picked up her purse. She opened the purse and took out the envelope that contained the CDs. Closing the purse and putting it down, she placed the envelope on the table in front of her, and picked up the phone. She punched in eleven digits. There was a pause and then the sound of her own phone in Oceanside ringing.

After three rings her service picked up the call. She waited for the announcement to end and then started to speak.

"James. I hope you get this. Did you get the files I sent? There's something very strange going on up here. I'm sorry about everything. I'm having dinner with the president of ABM, Arthur

Kazinski. If anything happens…Well I just wanted someone to know where I was…Call me."

She took the phone from her ear and held it a
moment before hanging up. It was noon in
California. He probably would not get the message 'til he got home later tonight. By then it
might be too late. Her thoughts were interrupted
by a knock at the door.

She went over to answer the door. Before she
opened it she checked through the peep hole to
see who it was. Standing on the other side of the
door was a young man in a green hotel uniform. It
was the clerk sent up from the front desk for her
package. She opened the door.

"Hi. Thanks for coming up so quickly." She did
not invite him in and he made no attempt to enter.

"Yes Ma'am. The front desk said you had something for safekeeping?"

"Yes. Just a minute. I'll get it." Monika left the
clerk at the door and went to get the envelope off
the sitting room table.

"Here you are." She returned and handed him
the Kraft envelope that was addressed to herself.
"I put my name on it." She pointed it out to the
clerk.

"If you could sign here please."

The clerk presented a small clipboard that had a
blank receipt form on it. She filled out her name,
signed the form and handed it back to him. The
clerk signed and ripped off Monika's copy and

gave it to her.

"There you are, Ma'am. Will there be anything else?" He was being polite but was also waiting for a tip.

"Oh. Yes. Just a minute."

She went back into the sitting room and took a two dollar coin out of her purse and returned to the clerk.

"Thank you." She handed the coin to him.

"Thank you." He made a slight bow, turned and walked away.

Monika closed the door and went back into the sitting room. She picked up her purse and put the receipt into it while she stood in front of the large picture window that overlooked the waterfront and the islands.

"I don't know what you're up to. But I'm going to find out." She was referring to Kazinski.

There were several hours before her dinner appointment. She decided to take a long bath and have a rest while she waited for the dinner date. Maybe she would still hear from Andrew. She wished he would call soon. She was becoming very worried.

●

The two men got out of the car and escorted Andrew over the unkempt shipping yard to a door in the warehouse. It was the only opening in the building that was not boarded up. There was no place Andrew could run to and there was no one around that could help him. He was at the mercy of these two men.

The first man unlocked the warehouse door and opened it.

"Hurry up," he ordered Andrew, who was standing a few yards away.

"Come on." The other man who was behind him pushed him forward. "This ain't no tour."

Andrew reluctantly went forward and entered into the warehouse.

Inside, the warehouse was pitch black. The only light available was the brightness that came from the outside through the open door. One of the men walked forward into the darkness. Andrew heard the sound of a main fuse box lever being pushed up into place. Within seconds of the sound, the warehouse ceiling lights began to flicker to life.

There was a long row of fluorescent lights suspended by wires from the ceiling, that ran down the center of the building. The place was very disorderly. There was a main aisle made out of poured concrete and a series of loading bay doors running along both sides of the warehouse. The structure reminded him of a very long railway platform. Each of the loading bay doors was closed tight. There were wood skids stacked by each door and general debris everywhere. The warehouse had not been used for a long time.

The man behind Andrew slammed the door to the outside. It shut with a loud bang, which startled Andrew.

"What's this all about?" Andrew asked both of them.

"Just shut up and come with us. You'll find out soon enough." The man behind him waved his gun at Andrew and indicated that he should move along behind the first man, who was walking down the platform. Andrew had no choice. He followed after the first man, with the second close on his heels.

The platform ran about three hundred feet. It was a long narrow area. The loading bays lined both sides all the way along its length. At one time this must have been one of the largest loading bays around. Andrew wondered what had been loaded here as they walked down its length to the opposite end of the building.

At the other end of the loading bay they came to a rusty metal staircase. The staircase led up one flight to what appeared to be an office that overlooked the whole area. The three of them went up the stairs.

On the second floor there was a small landing and a door to an office. The first man opened the door and, as he entered the office, felt for the light switch on the left side of the jamb. He turned on the lights. They all went in.

The room was spartan. There was an old grey metal desk that had seen better days and a couple of chairs. There was a calendar on the wall next to a five by eight cork bulletin board. The calendar was out of date and displayed a pornographic picture of a large-breasted woman. There was a dirty glass ashtray with old cigarette butts in it. Placed next to the ashtray was a black old-style dial phone.

"Sit down over there and don't say a word," the man who had been behind him ordered Andrew.

"But what do you want?" Andrew pleaded.

The man threw a punch that hit Andrew squarely on the left jaw. Andrew fell to the floor in pain. He had been hit pretty hard. He gingerly rubbed his face with his right hand.

"I said sit down and shut up!" The man was menacing.

Andrew slowly pulled himself up and sat down in one of the chairs that was near to the bulletin board. He was subdued. His jaw hurt. He was afraid and bewildered. Who were these men? What did they want? Why had he been brought here? Who was behind all of this? These men were obviously thugs that were working for someone else. Kazinski? He wondered if this had anything to do with Monika's phone call to ABM. He hoped that she was okay. She would be waiting for his call.

The man who had hit Andrew picked up the phone and dialed a number.

"Hello sir. We have him here." The man spoke to someone over the phone. His face was impassive as he listened to his instructions.

"..
...."

"Yes sir. What about Ms. Queller?"

Andrew heard Monika's name but kept his eyes carefully lowered. It had to be Kazinski on the other end. Who else could it be? Somehow Kazinski was involved. Both he and Monika were in grave danger. He did not let on his surprise to the two men.

"What time?" The man on the phone checked his wristwatch as he was being given instructions over the phone.

"............................"

"We can arrange that." He smiled slightly as he listened to further orders.

"..."

"Yes. We will." The man hung up the phone and turned to Andrew. "It seems we are going to have a little dinner party." He laughed and picked up the phone and dialed another number. Andrew did not respond.

So that was it. Kazinski was involved. Something must have gone wrong. Somehow Monika must have alerted Kazinski to their suspicions. Whatever it was it had pushed Kazinski to react very quickly. It must be something very important to get such a rapid reaction.

Why was he still alive? Why had he been picked up and brought here? How had Kazinski made the connection between him and Monika? There were many unanswered questions buzzing through Andrew's mind as he came to all these realizations. Whatever the reason, he was glad to be alive. They obviously needed him that way for now. From what the man on the phone had said, Monika was going to be here at some point. Whether it was willingly or by force he did not know. He hoped an opportunity would arise that would help them both escape. He would wait for that appropriate moment before he made any move. He wasn't sure what that move would be under such conditions, but he would be ready when the opportunity presented itself to him. Right now all he could do was wait and do as he was told.

●

High up in the sky, James' plane was making good headway. James was very agitated about Monika's safety and couldn't wait to touch down.

"Good afternoon ladies and gentlemen. This is the Captain…"

The voice of the pilot was very laid back and relaxed as it sounded over the noise of the jet engines.

"It looks like we will be arriving earlier than we thought. We've had some good tail winds along this journey. We expect to be on the ground in Toronto around six-forty local time. I'm told the weather there is warm and sunny. High of 26

Celsius or about 80 degrees Fahrenheit. Sorry for the interruption. I hope you're having a pleasant flight." The message ended as abruptly as it had started.

James felt a little more at ease. He was happy to be ahead of schedule. The minute he cleared customs he would call Monika's hotel to make sure she was alright.

The CDs were very strong evidence of ABM's illicit conduct. At the very least, the information they contained would cause a dramatic decline in the value of ABM's stock. Perhaps even threaten ABM's future. The CDs implicated the company president, Arthur Kazinski, in the wrongdoing. He had a copy of the files that Monika had sent with him. He would show these to the RCMP officers meeting him at the airport.

The RCMP had been advised of ABM's illegal actions and had been requested to watch out for Monika. James hoped that she had not done anything foolish. He fervently hoped that she was not directly involved. ABM would do anything to prevent the CDs from falling into the wrong hands. They would most certainly kill, if it was required to keep things quiet.

Monika had stumbled upon an international crime. She had, whether knowingly or not, done the right thing by sending the files to him. Now the information was in the hands of the authorities. ABM would not be able to continue in these covert activities. The only concern that James had was whether or not ABM knew this fact. If they did know, they would try to cover up their conspiracy and make it difficult for them to be prosecuted. If they were not aware of the authorities' possession of the files, they would dispose of anyone who had knowledge of the conspiracy in hopes of keeping it concealed. They would act quickly to protect the contents of the CDs. They would not anticipate that the information on them could or would be e-mailed to him. In any event, they still would not let any individuals newly aware of their contents survive.

James looked out the plane window next to his seat. It seemed so peaceful and secure here above the clouds. He prayed that he would get to Monika in time to protect her from the dangers he knew lay below.

Chapter 11

In the Lobby of the Weston two men came in and sat down near the front entrance. One sat directly on the sofa across from the entrance doors and the other sat on the sofa that was closer to the west end of the lobby near the elevators. They were both very clean-cut and wore business attire. Their shoes were highly polished. The one sitting in front of the main entrance was in his thirties. The other appeared to be in his late twenties. They were both slim and fit looking. They had the look of the military. They each sat and tried to act nonchalant. One picked up the complimentary newspaper from the table in front of him and pretended to be interested in it. It was obvious that he was watching for someone. The other was sitting and scrutinizing people as they walked by. This one pulled out his wallet from his jacket pocket and took out a small photograph and examined it. It was Monika's picture. After he had committed her likeness to memory, he put the picture back into the wallet and back into his jacket pocket.

Both men sat there and made themselves comfortable. They did not look at each other but kept focused on the elevators, lobby and entrance.

●

Monika was dressed. She had taken a long hot bath and relaxed while she waited for Andrew to call. The phone never rang once. It was almost time for her to go down to the lobby and meet the limousine that Kazinski was sending for her. She had butterflies in her stomach. Why hadn't Andrew called her? What had happened to him? Was he involved in her being chased today? She had many doubts in her mind. She did not want to believe that Andrew had fooled her or that he had tricked her into searching Kazinski's office, placing her in jeopardy. There had to be a reason why he had not called. Maybe he was hurt. What would she do if he was hurt and had no way to contact her? What would she do then? She had taken the CDs and was now in the middle of a bad situation. How was she going to extricate herself?

All these questions went through her mind as she finished dressing. She stood in front of the bedroom mirror to give herself a final once over.

She was wearing a black 'A' line dress. It was simple but looked very pretty on her. It was the only dinner dress she had brought with her. She had planned to buy something else while on her stay here in Emerald City. The fashions here were a lot more European in design than American. She wanted to pick up a couple of things that she wouldn't be able to find in California.

Her shoes were black patent leather and of the current style in their 'clunky' appearance, but went well with the outfit. Her hair was pinned up, highlighting her cheekbones and drawing attention to her blue eyes.

"Well, are you ready for this?" she asked her image in the mirror. "Cause I don't think I am."

She checked her watch: 6:55. The limousine would be downstairs at seven. She could not put the inevitable off any longer.

Turning away from the mirror, she left the bedroom and picked up her small black purse from the table in the sitting room. The purse completed her look, as she flung it over her left shoulder and walked to the door of the room. She placed her hand on the door handle and opened it. She paused and gave the room a quick check, then walked out of the room. The door automatically closed behind her. She went down the hall and pushed the call button for the elevator. She was the only person in the hall. She tapped the fingers of her right hand nervously against her right upper leg as she awaited the elevator. She gave her watch one last check. It was 6:58.

●

James' plane landed early. By the time he disembarked it was 6:45. He walked down the long narrow enclosed gang plank into the same corridors that Monika had walked upon her arrival here just a few days before. As he had no bags, he was anxious to get to customs, meet his Canadian cohorts and call Monika at the hotel.

James came to the main room where the immigration officers sat in their booths. He went up to the first booth and officer he saw that was available.

"Passport?"

"I don't have it with me. Here's my driver's license." James understood the procedure but was agitated by its slowness. He kept checking the time on his watch as the officer went through his usual routine.

"Citizenship?" the officer nonchalantly asked as he typed James' information into his computer terminal. He was suspicious of James and was going to check him thoroughly.

"U.S." James answered in a tone that was trying to speed things up.

"Purpose of your stay?" The officer asked as he half watched his monitor and James.

"Business."

"What type of business?" The officer became more interested.

Before he could answer, James' information came up on the monitor. There was an alert posted to the screen.

"Mr. Anstey? Could you wait a moment please?" The officer's tone became more deferential.

"Sure." James knew what had happened. The message on the screen had been tagged to his name by the RCMP. They were expecting him.

The officer picked up the phone and spoke into the receiver. James could not make out what was being said. It did not concern him. He was more worried about getting through all this red tape and calling Monika. After the officer hung up the phone he sat staring at James without saying a word. James thought he was acting a little strange.

From behind the opaque glass wall that surrounded the customs area, a figure could be seen approaching. Part of the wall was a sliding doorway. The doorway was off to one side of the customs officers. Neither James nor the officer could see the approach. A man in his forties wearing a dark suit entered the immigration area through the sliding door on the opposite side of the room and crossed over to the booth where James was standing.

"Mr. Anstey?" the man asked as he came up to James, who was not expecting him.

"Yes?" James turned to face the man who was offering his hand.

"Craig Jeneau. Royal Canadian Mounted Police. We've been expecting you." Jeneau smiled as they shook hands. He had a slight accent. James identified it as French.

"Thank you, Mark." Jeneau spoke to the immigration officer.

"No problem." The officer smiled.

"Shall we get out of here?" Jeneau addressed James.

Jeneau led James across the room to the sliding door that he had come through and tapped upon the glass. Moments later the door slid open and both he and James left the immigration area and stepped out into the main terminal of the airport. There was a guard seated to the left of the sliding door.

"Thanks." Jeneau acknowledged the guard as he and James passed by.

Jeneau and James walked through the arrivals area towards the exit. The arrivals area was a huge open room. Farther down was the gate where the regular passengers, once cleared through customs, exited to be met by their loved ones. The door that James and Jeneau had come through was about fifty feet away from the main crowd of people.

Beyond the waiting area was the outer wall of the terminal, which faced out onto the arrivals roadway. The outer wall was supported by large square pillars. The spaces between the pillars were filled with ceiling to floor solid pane windows. Through the windows James could see all the arrival's traffic: buses, cars and limousines. There were many cars on the roadway. There were a few porters standing on the sidewalk outside and people loading bags into their cars. The area was particularly busy with the arrival of James' flight.

"We got the information from your office. It sounds pretty much like science fiction. How did you guys stumble upon it?" Jeneau spoke with James as they walked across the arrivals area to the sliding door that led to the outside of the terminal. "I'm parked out here on the road," he added for James' orientation.

"It fell into our lap. We weren't investigating 'til we got this tip."

James was not paying much attention to their conversation, but was on guard. It was a natural way of behaving when dealing with non-domestic agencies. Why tell them anything more than was minimally required to get the job done? It was the standard fare exchanged between investigating agents and both men expected this type of 'holding back.' It was all part of the game of intelligence agencies.

"That's a bit of luck."

Jeneau went through the sliding door first, leading the way. He knew there was more to this case than James was letting on. Why else all the rush? Normally a request would have been made from the foreign agency to the RCMP to do preliminary investigations and then report. All that had been passed over and they had gone directly to field work. There was something much more urgent about this case.

"Is there a phone nearby? I need to make a call." James changed the subject.

"To your girlfriend? Ms. Queller?" Jeneau smiled. He saw the look of surprise upon James' face. "We have our sources as well. I have sent two of my men to her hotel to watch out for her."

"Is she alright?"

"I don't know. We haven't spotted her yet."

James hesitated a moment and then decided to let Jeneau know the truth. There was no point in risking Monika's safety because of the 'game'.

"She's the informant. She sent us the files on ABM." James gave Jeneau the information that he had suspected. "I think she's in danger."

"Don't worry, my men are the best." Jeneau appreciated the straightforwardness. He understood now that this was more than 'business as usual.' It involved family. He would do whatever he could to help James.

They walked along the sidewalk and came up to a parked brown four-door sedan. It was unlocked. There was a small antenna sticking out of the trunk. The car had the distinctive look of the undercover police. Jeneau got in the driver's side and James the front passenger side.

James noticed a familiar aroma. The inside of the car smelled of coffee. There was a small white bag on the bench seat and a half-eaten donut on it.

"That's my dinner." Jeneau moved the bag and donut out of James' way. They both sat and closed their doors.

Jeneau then picked up the car phone which was attached to the lower dashboard.

"We can call the hotel from here." He punched in the hotel phone number and handed the phone to James. "Just push send."

"Thanks."

James took the phone with his left hand and pushed send with his right forefinger. He switched the phone to his right hand and put it to his ear. He checked the time on the wristwatch on his left forearm: 6:57.

The phone rang several times and then was answered by the front desk of the hotel.

"Weston Hotel."

"1711 South please." James asked.

"I'll connect you sir."

●

The phone started to ring in Monika's room just as she was walking away from her room toward the elevator. She did not hear the ringing. She was distracted by the sound of the elevator arriving and the doors opening. She got into the elevator. There was no one else aboard. She turned around and faced the doors as they closed. There was an uneasy look on her face.

●

James let the phone ring until the hotel operator came back on the line.

"Sorry there's no answer. May I take a message?" It was a female operator.

"No. Thanks. I'll try later." James disconnected.

"No luck?" Jeneau noted James' disappointment. "She's probably out for dinner. We can go straight to the hotel if you like?" Jeneau had already been briefed by his superiors via the information that James' office had given to them. He was put in charge of the investigation and told to help James any way he could.

James sat silent for a moment. He had an intuition that he was trying to comprehend. He trusted his intuitions. They had always been right and constant. In his line of work it was important to have such an ally.

"Do you mind if I make another call?" he asked Jeneau.

"Go ahead. It's the company phone." Jeneau made himself comfortable as James punched in the number.

James put the phone to his ear and listened as the phone was answered by an answering machine.

"Hi. After the beep leave me your name and number and I'll get back to you soon."

It was Monika's voice. James punched in a code using the keypad on the cellular phone. There was a loud tone and then an automated voice message:

"You have…one…message."

The voice filled in the blanks of the otherwise standard message in a very choppy computerized tonality. There was another short tone and the message was played back:

"James. I hope you get this. Did you get the files I sent? There's something very strange going on up here. I'm sorry about everything. I'm having dinner with the president of ABM, Arthur Kazinski, if anything happens…Well I just wanted someone to know where I was…Call me."

It was Monika's voice. She sounded a little afraid and lonely.

"What's wrong?" Jeneau questioned James. He noted James' troubled expression.

James disconnected from the service and put the receiver back in its place on the lower dashboard.

"A message from my girlfriend. She's going to meet Kazinski. Damn."

Jeneau understood the danger. Kazinski was well known to him. If what the files contained was true, then James' girlfriend was putting herself in the center of real trouble.

"Did she say where?"

"No."

"Let's get to the hotel and see what we can find. I can check in with my men from there."

"Yeah." James nodded his acceptance.

Jeneau started the car and pulled out into the traffic. They were only twenty minutes away from the hotel.

●

Monika rode down in silence. The elevator stopped at three floors on its way to the lobby. Each time new passengers got on, she checked to see who they were. She was looking for anyone who might be out of place. Someone who was not really a hotel guest; someone who was following her. Each group of people that got on the elevator seemed legitimate.

The elevator was quite crowded by the time it arrived at the main lobby. Monika did not exit right away. She waited. She wanted to be last to get out. She was trying to appear normal and calm. She nervously scanned the area as she stepped from the elevator into the west end of the lobby.

The lobby was filled with the chatter of hotel guests. In the background, piano music was coming from the lobby lounge. Monika walked out into the main thoroughfare and headed for the main entrance. She did not see anything that was unusual—though she wasn't sure she knew exactly what unusual meant. She walked by the sitting area in front of the lobby lounge and headed for the revolving entrance doors. Once at the doors, she peered out into the driveway. Kazinski's limousine was parked directly in front of the doors. The chauffeur was standing at the rear of the limousine checking each party as they came through the hotel's main entry. Monika pasted a smile on her face. She walked up to the main doors and exited the hotel.

"Ms. Queller," the chauffeur called out on recognizing his rider. He directed her the fifteen feet from the lobby exit to the passenger door, opened it and guided her inside.

Monika got into the car and sat clutching her purse close to her. Her heart was racing. She hoped that she had done the right thing by accepting the dinner invitation, although there was nothing else she could do. She hoped that James got her message. Just in case something…she did not finish the thought. The chauffeur had gotten into the car. They drove off down the driveway and away from the hotel.

●

The two men had spotted Monika the second she appeared in the lobby. They carefully signaled each other and had gotten up from their seats to follow her. Monika had not noticed either of them as she had made her way to the main entrance.

The two men kept a safe distance from her as they followed her to the revolving doors. They joined each other at the doors, and pretended that they were looking out for someone in the main covered drive of the hotel. They had each watched as she had gotten into the limousine. Once the limousine had started to leave, they hurried out through the revolving doors to a car that was parked in the short term waiting area. They both quickly got in as the limousine pulled away from the main entrance. They were under very strict orders not to lose the girl after they had found her. They were to keep her in view and follow wherever she went. They were to report and not to interfere unless it was a matter of life and death.

They pulled out to follow after the black limousine. They decided not to report their sighting of the girl right away. They wanted to get a better idea of where the limousine was going. So far they had been lucky. They did not believe that either the girl or the driver of the limousine were aware that they were being followed. They kept a safe distance behind so as not to raise any suspicions.

Chapter 12

S he wondered where she was being taken. The limousine turned right on the main road in front of the hotel and headed east. They passed by a condominium highrise complex that had a large sculpture in front. The sculpture resembled two oversized egg beaters and, instead of turning on the street that the egg beaters cornered, the street that would have led to the expressway, the limousine continued straight along the harborfront away from the downtown business corridor.

Monika sat silently observing as they drove. They passed the Toronto Daily News building on the left and the Port of Toronto buildings on the right. Running along the south side of the road was an old railway shunting line.

About a mile from the hotel, the buildings were less impressive or grand than the main city structures. Monika was amazed at how quickly the glow of Emerald City faded. It was as if the city had exuded a magical power that had abruptly ended here at this point, and the seedy underbelly of the city was revealed. This part of town was less developed. It was a more industrial area; a part of town that tourists never saw.

The limousine continued. Soon it came to a curve in the road that led northward. Ahead, and overtop, was the expressway. The limousine stopped at a set of lights at the intersection directly underneath the expressway.

Running under the raised expressway was another highway that, like the arteries beneath the skin, was linked and flowed in harmony with its protective structure above, never straying beyond the boundaries of this skin.

The lights changed. The limousine crossed this subterranean highway and about fifty feet farther northward, went under an old railway bridge which was very dirty and in need of repair.

On the other side of the railway bridge and to the left, were a series of low-income housing apartments. Their red brick ten-story or so height dominated the street on its western side. There was not a person to be seen. The area had a ghostly feel to it.

On the right was an old run-down industrial warehousing district. There were large black tanks surrounded by a barbed wire fence. Behind the tanks was an old six-story fieldstone building that resembled, and might well have originally been, an old prison from the eighteen hundreds.

The limousine turned right on the next street it came to. Monika caught a glimpse of the street name—Mill Street.

This part of town that the street ran through was the worst she had yet seen in Emerald City. Both sides of the street were lined with uninhabited, boarded-up old buildings. These buildings were all of the same period and design. They were all made of red brick and varied between four and six stories. They dated back to the early nineteen hundreds and had probably at one time been the pride of the industrial life of this city. Now they were dilapidated, sooty, crumbling wrecks that no one seemed to care about. There was a haunting quality to them as they rigidly stood as a testament to their younger prowess; a prowess that was now long forgotten. They silently stood as erect as they could—like old men trying to retain whatever dignity remained to their weakening and decaying physicality.

The limousine passed by these buildings and came to the next intersection. On the northwest corner was an old ironmonger's yard. Sheets of metal formed a makeshift fence around the property.

On the southwest corner was a vacant lot overgrown with weeds. Evidence that a structure had once stood there, but had long ago been torn down, could be seen.

On the southwest corner was the Canari Café. It was the only place that seemed to have any life to it amongst all these boarded-up and neglected buildings. It was amazing that it had managed to survive here in this graveyard.

The limousine turned north and immediately into the driveway of the property on the northeast corner.

The property had a five foot chain link fence surrounding it. On the fence at the main entrance was a 'FOR LEASE or SALE' sign and the name of the realty company to contact. Monika could only make out the front of the property. She strained to see the property through the car window. She wanted to better know where she was being taken. She was very uneasy about being here.

There was an old building of a more contemporary design with fifties style and color brick work on the property. It was an old warehouse of some sort. This was obviously the main office area of the building and it rose two stories high. It was the only building in the immediate area that seemed to have been only recently let go.

"Hey. Where are we going? Why have you

brought me here?" she shouted to the chauffeur from her back seat, but he did not hear her. The glass partition was closed between them. She sat back in nervous frustration. All she could do was wait and see what would happen next. The chauffeur had obviously been ordered to ignore her questions and merely deliver her here.

The limousine pulled up and stopped in front of the main doors of the abandoned warehouse. Monika's heart raced and her eyes were wide open with growing apprehension. The chauffeur got out of the car and came round to the passenger side nearest the entry. He took hold of the door handle and opened the door. Monika hesitated. She was not anxious to get out into this unknown desolate place. She was not sure what she should do. This was obviously not a place to have dinner.

As she sat there wondering whether to remain seated or to get out, the front doors of the warehouse opened—out stepped a beaming Kazinski.

"Right on time!" he bellowed with a smile. The trip had only taken eight minutes from the hotel.

Monika saw and heard Kazinski as he approached, but did not respond.

"I hope you don't mind this little detour before dinner." Kazinski was now at the limousine and leaning into the passenger compartment speaking to her.

Monika felt a little less tense now that Kazinski

had mentioned that this was only a detour and that he intended to have dinner. But why bring her here?

"I have someone I'd like you to meet before we go on. Please." He gallantly offered Monika his helping hand to get out from the limousine.

There was nothing that Monika could do but comply with his wishes and hope to get out of here as quickly as possible. She drew in a breath and, as she accepted his help by taking his hand, commented. "I hope it's not going to be too long. I'm famished."

Kazinski chuckled.

"No. It should only be a couple of minutes. Not more."

Monika got out of the limousine and was escorted by Kazinski into the building. The chauffeur closed the door and got back into the limousine to wait. The engine was still running.

The inside of the building was lit by old, dim fluorescent lighting. The tubes gave off a yellowed glow. They entered into a large room. It had been at one time a large reception area, but there was no longer any furniture or other decoration. They walked through the empty space to a door on the opposite side of the room from the outside entrance.

"This was our original plant when we started in the late fifties. Seems like only yesterday that this place was bustling with life. We moved out into the new place in the early sixties. Now we're planning on moving again. Business has been better than expected."

Kazinski gave her a brief history. He was very charming and polite, but Monika sensed that he had something on his mind. Kazinski was not what he appeared to be, and the reason for being here in this old warehouse was more than just a social call on some acquaintance. He had the demeanor of a carnival con man. Underneath his thousand dollar suit and fine cologne was nothing but a rogue.

"Why haven't you sold this place before?"

Monika engaged him in conversation in hopes of building some sort of rapport between them that might come in useful and protect her from whatever lay ahead.

"Good question. We probably should have disposed of this property long ago. I suppose it was just sentimental. I always thought we could turn it into a museum—a shrine to the crusader of the computer age." He smiled as he thought of what a glorious tribute that would be to ABM and himself.

He had taken the company over during its difficult period and made it into the international success that it was today. If it had not been for his leadership, ABM might only be a third rate competitor today.

"Now with prices down, we couldn't get what

we want. It is an irony isn't it?" He turned to see Monika's reaction.

"Yeah." Monika shyly smiled and agreed. She found Kazinski to be a pompous jerk.

They crossed to the door and Kazinski opened it.

"After you."

"Thank you." Monika entered with trepidation.

The door opened into a large warehouse. There were a series of garage-like doors that lined both sides of a long platform. It was some sort of shipping area. It was very dirty. It was cluttered with garbage and broken, discolored cardboard shipping boxes. There were wood skids, that had been left lying around since the closure of the warehouse, next to several of the loading bays.

"This way." Kazinski showed Monika to the open metal staircase that led to a second story office above them.

"So who is it that you want me to meet?" Monika pried as she started up the stairs with Kazinski close behind her.

"I wouldn't want to spoil the surprise. It won't be much longer now."

They came to the top of the metal stairs and the landing in front of an office. Monika waited as Kazinski came and took the lead. He walked over to the door to the office, put his hand upon the handle and pulled the door open.

"Please." Kazinski indicated that she should go

in. Monika reluctantly acceded to his wishes and walked into the room.

It was a tiny little office. There was a bulletin board on the far wall with a nude girl calendar upon it. A metal desk was against the wall. Three men were in the room. Monika recognized one of the men as her pursuer from earlier that day. The man smiled knowingly at her. Another man was standing next to him. She did not recognize him but assumed by their similar dress that they worked together and for Kazinski. The third man was seated in a chair and had his back turned to her and Kazinski. There was a single thin rope securing him to the chair. Monika became flustered, but did not react. The seated man who was casually dressed was much younger and smaller than the two larger suited men standing guard over him.

Kazinski entered into the room and closed the door. He indicated that the men should turn the man on the chair around to face them.

As they turned him around, Kazinski said, "Ms. Queller. I'd like you to meet…"

The man was turned around. Monika's eyes met his.

"…Mr. Ambrose." Kazinski enjoyed her surprise. He noted that they recognized each other.

"Oh. I see that you are already acquainted with each other. Well…that's a surprise." Kazinski turned to face Monika. His tone became menacing.

"Isn't it."

●

Jeneau's men managed to follow the limousine without any difficulty. They had kept a safe distance behind and out of sight of the driver. When the limousine had pulled into the abandoned warehouse, they had pulled up out of sight near the scrap metal yard on the northwest side of the street. They were able to keep their car out of sight behind the sheet metal fence that lined the property. Through a ripped section of the sheet metal, they were able to just make out what was going on over at the warehouse that the limousine had stopped in front of. They were not able to see into the limousine because of its tinted windows. They watched as the driver got out of the limousine and went to the passenger door and opened it.

"Hey look. There." The man in the passenger seat pointed out for his partner to observe.

"Oh yeah. I see. It looks like Kazinski."

"Yeah. Funny place for him to be at this time of day. Don't you think?"

"Yeah. Maybe there is something to all this?"

They both fell silent as they watched Kazinski come out of the building and walk towards the limousine. He was greeting someone. It had to be Monika. They watched as Kazinski came over to the limousine and leaned into it through the open door. The driver was standing dispassionately behind him.

They watched as Kazinski helped someone out of the vehicle. It was Monika. She appeared to be afraid and reluctant to go with Kazinski. He seemed to have some power over her. They walked into the warehouse.

After Monika and Kazinski disappeared into the building, the driver closed the door and got back into the limousine. They could see by the exhaust that the limousine's engine was running. It remained in place in front of the warehouse doors. The vehicle did not drive off. Obviously it was waiting—but for what?

"We'd better call this one in and see what Jeneau wants us to do." The man on the passenger side pulled out his cellular phone while he spoke and punched in a number. He put the phone to his ear and waited for an answer. Both men kept their eyes on the warehouse and the limousine.

●

Jeneau and James were on the highway en route to the hotel when the cellular phone rang. Jeneau stretched over with his right hand and took the phone from its position under the dash.

"Jeneau." he said in a business tone as he listened.

" ....
....
....
.... "

"And she went inside?" Jeneau nodded to James as he spoke into the phone.

"............"

"Stay there. If they leave let me know right away."

"...

.........................?" There was a question being asked.

"Then one of you follow them and one find out what's inside that warehouse. Okay?" Jeneau directed, then confirmed with the party on the other end of the call.

"..."

Jeneau hung up the phone.

"It seems that your girlfriend is with Kazinski. They have gone into an abandoned warehouse," he informed James.

"Where? Is she okay?"

"Not far from the hotel in the east side of the city. My men are there. She isn't hurt." He paused and looked into James' eyes. "She will be alright, my friend." He smiled reassuringly.

James appreciated Jeneau's kindness. He was beginning to like this guy, "So what are we going to do?"

"We can go right to the warehouse. It will be about half an hour before we get there. My men will watch and wait outside unless they suspect something."

"What do you mean?"

"The limousine that your girlfriend arrived in is waiting outside the front of the warehouse. Its engine is running. I think that they will not be long inside."

"Can't we get there any faster?"

"We can try."

Jeneau leaned over to the left side of the lower dashboard. As he kept one eye on the road and his right hand on the steering wheel, he took out a portable emergency light with his left. It began to flash as he activated it and placed it on the driver's side of the outside roof of the car. A long extension cord ran from the light and into the car. It was connected to the electrical wiring under the dash.

"Let's go, eh?" Jeneau smiled. He lived for this sort of thing. He put his foot to the floor and the car rapidly accelerated.

●

"Andrew?" Monika confirmed Kazinski's suspicions. She called out and moved towards Andrew.

"Monika. What…"

Andrew tried to get out of the chair but was restrained by the rope and Kazinski's men. He did not finish his sentence.

"How nice." Kazinski interrupted Andrew. "So you are acquainted. Monika you disappoint me." He directed his comment to her. "I had hoped that you weren't involved in all…" he waved his hand, "…this."

Monika did not say a thing.

"So you did take the CDs."

Kazinski crossed over in front of her and stood very uncomfortably close to her. Monika could smell his body odor. She backed away and one of Kazinski's men stepped up and grabbed hold of her, preventing her from moving any farther.

"CDs?" Andrew queried out loud.

"Yes. I found them in his office, but I haven't been able to see what's on them. I think it's important." Monika glared at Kazinski as she answered. The ruse was up. There was no point in pretending anymore.

"You're correct. They are important. It is a pity that you got involved in all this. Now I will have to deal with you as I did with his father." Kazinski grinned as he aimed this part of his sentence to Andrew.

"You bastard." Andrew tugged at his restraints without success, in an attempt to get at Kazinski.

"Shut him up. I've heard enough from him." Kazinski ordered the man restraining Andrew. The man put his large hand around Andrew's lower face and muzzled him.

"Now Ms. Queller. The CDs. Where are they? I'd like them back, and if you and Mr. Ambrose have any hope of surviving…" he pointed out the obvious threat that they were under, "…you'd better give them back to me—now." He gave Monika a penetrating stare.

Monika was sure that Kazinski would not let them live after he got the CDs, but she did not let him know her thoughts. She was glad that she had not brought them with her.

"I gave them to the police," she bluffed.

Kazinski regarded her and then his men. "Nice try, but I don't believe you. George. Check her."

The man that was holding onto Monika threw her around and began to pat her down. He was a perverse individual. He started by patting her down from her shoulders and then in and around her brassiere and breasts. He enjoyed the touching. Monika tried to pull away, but it did not stop his groping. In fact he seemed to enjoy it more as she physically protested. He looked her straight in the eyes as he fondled her and slowly moved down with his hands to search all of her.

Monika did not close her eyes, but defiantly stared back at him as his hands traversed her abdomen and slid under the hem of her dress. She squirmed at his unwanted touch. It made her feel unclean. George's hand slid into her panties and she felt his rough touch upon her. She protested again. George grinned and went further 'til he felt the warm space between the inside of her thighs. It did not last long, but it was long enough. Monika pulled back and forced his hand out of her panties and dress. She gave him a chilling menacing look.

"That's enough George. Check her purse. We

don't want to upset Ms. Queller too much."
Kazinski had enjoyed watching George's search
and Monika's reaction.

George grabbed Monika's purse and undid its
clasp. He turned the purse upside down and emp-
tied its contents onto the metal table. Everything
noisily fell out: lipstick, keys, make-up, pen,
etcetera. All the things that men are always surprised to see that a woman carries. George threw
the purse down next to the items and rifled
through everything. There were clearly no CDs,
but there was an odd piece of paper that did not
seem to fit in with the purse's belongings.

As George was going through the items,
Monika tried not to look too closely. She had seen
the receipt fall amongst the items onto the table.
She did not want to give it away by staring and
drawing George's eye to it. George did not need
her assistance. He found it on his own. She
remained expressionless as he picked up the piece
of paper, examined it and regarded her.

"Sir. I think this might be what we are looking
for."

The receipt had several digits on it, along with
the Weston Hotel stamped upon it in dark green
ink. It was a claim check for something being
kept in safekeeping at the hotel. George realized
this fact as he presented it to Kazinski.

Kazinski took hold of the receipt and, like
George, examined it closely.

"Yes. I think you might be right." He smiled and spoke to Monika. "Now. What could this possibly be the claim check for, eh?"

Monika did not answer.

Kazinski stared at her. He was testing her and watched her uncomfortable reaction while he waved the claim stub in front of her face.

"I don't believe that Ms. Queller gave the CDs to the police."

Though staring at Monika and watching her silent facial reaction, he was speaking to his men in the room.

"I think she has put them in safekeeping at the hotel."

He now spoke pointedly to Monika. "What do you think, Monika?"

He brought his face very close to hers when he posed this last question.

Monika said nothing, but her silence said everything Kazinski needed to know.

Kazinski backed away.

"I think we had better take a ride to the hotel and see what this…" he again waved the receipt, "…belongs to."

"They won't give it to you," Monika blurted out.

Kazinski turned around. "You're right. You'll be coming along."

"What about Andrew?"

"He'll remain here. After I get the CDs George

and Phil will let him go." He changed his tone back to charming. "All I'm interested in is getting the CDs, nothing else. Without them you have nothing."

Monika did not believe him, but it was the only thing she could do. She had to go with him to the hotel. It would buy a little more time for both Andrew and herself. Maybe something would happen that would help them both. If she didn't go, then both their fates were decided here and now.

"How do I know you won't just kill us?" Monika played the part.

"Ms. Queller." Kazinski came over to her. "I'm not a monster." He raised his hand to Monika's left cheek. Monika became tense and tried not to display her disgust at his move to touch her.

"All I want are the CDs. Besides…" He stroked her check with the back of his left hand index finger. "…I like the way you write." He seductively smiled as he looked into her large blue eyes. Monika looked away from his perverse glare. Kazinski grinned. He was not insulted by her aversion. He had her where he wanted.

During all of these events Andrew had been watching helplessly from his chair. He had not been able to speak out because of Phil's muzzle hold on him. He tried to communicate with Monika through his eyes, but she had ignored him.

There was an awkward silence as Kazinski regarded Monika. He liked more than her writing. After he had the CDs he would not kill her; at least not right away. First he would 'get to know her' then he would dispose of her. As far as Andrew Ambrose was concerned, he had already caused far too much trouble. He would be killed the minute the CDs were returned. Monika need not know any of this. It would only complicate matters. Kazinski's primary concern was to retrieve the CDs before they fell into the wrong hands. It was fortunate that he was dealing with these two amateurs. Had they been smarter they would have gone straight to the authorities with the CDs. That would have been the only way to have protected their lives. Kazinski turned his back to Monika and gave new orders to his men.

"Phil. You and George stay here with Ambrose. Ms. Queller and I will go to the hotel to get the CDs."

He looked back at Monika and then back to Phil. Monika could not see Kazinski's facial expressions. She could only hear his voice.

"I'll call when I have them. Then you can let him go." Kazinski winked at Phil to indicate that he was not to let Andrew go, but to kill him.

Andrew began to squirm and make noise upon seeing the deceit. Phil grabbed harder onto him, forcing him to stop the commotion.

"Don't hurt him," Monika pleaded as Phil manhandled Andrew.

"He'll be okay. " Kazinski now faced her. "I don't think he likes the idea of being left behind." He spoke to Andrew who was still muzzled and writhing. "Don't you worry. We won't be long."

That being said, Kazinski crossed the room to the door and opened it.

"Come along Monika."

Monika quickly picked up her purse and shoved the things back into it as Kazinski waited at the door. While she was repackaging her purse she visually connected with Andrew to let him know that she had understood and that she had a plan. Andrew was relieved that she had not been fooled. Though he continued to squirm and protest, he was a little less afraid inside.

Monika crossed the room and left with Kazinski. She prayed everything would work out; that she was doing the right thing by leaving Andrew there with those two thugs.

With Monika in front, she and Kazinski went back down the metal staircase to the warehouse floor. Kazinski escorted her, by taking hold of her arm, into the reception area and out the front door. He did not want to take the chance of her getting away.

When the chauffeur saw them exit, he sprang out of the limousine and ran to open the passenger door. Kazinski pushed Monika and got in beside her. The chauffeur closed the door and went back to his driver's side. He did not comment on Kazinski's harsh treatment of Monika. After the driver's door closed, the limousine sat idling in front of the warehouse entrance for a few moments longer. Kazinski was giving the chauffeur his directions. The chauffeur put the car in gear and the limousine pulled forward, away from the warehouse doors and out onto the city street.

Chapter 13

Jeneau's men watched as Kazinski and Monika came out of the warehouse and got into the limousine. They were both a little surprised that Kazinski was getting into the vehicle with Monika so soon after she had arrived at the building. She couldn't have been inside for more than ten minutes. This was an unusual development. The man in the driver's seat picked up the car phone and punched in the number for Jeneau. This was a development that needed to be reported immediately. ●

Jeneau and James were fifteen minutes away from the warehouse. They had made better time using the emergency light, but it was the tail end of rush hour in the city and the traffic was heavy. It would take longer than Jeneau had anticipated to get to the warehouse. The phone rang. Jeneau picked up the receiver.

"Hello?"

"..
....
...."

"Okay Tom. You go ahead and follow them. Have Craig investigate the warehouse. We'll go straight to the hotel. Let me know when you find out where they're going." Jeneau hung up. It had been a quick conversation.

"They're on the move. Kazinski and your girl-friend got into the limousine and left the ware-house. We'll go to the hotel. Hopefully by then we'll have an idea where they are going."

James nodded his understanding.

●

The conversation had been brief. Tom hung up the phone as the limousine drove to the corner of Cherry and Mill Streets. Both men ducked below their car window so as not to be seen as the lim-ousine turned and came in their direction going west on Mill Street.

"Craig. You go in and see what's inside the warehouse. I'll keep tailing them." Tom spoke as both men hid.

Once the limousine passed by, both men care-fully rose up. Tom started the car and Craig got out. He ran across to the sheet metal fence of the scrap yard and stood away from the view of the warehouse and the limousine. He signaled his partner to indicate that everything was okay

Seeing that Craig was in position, Tom turned the car one hundred and eighty degrees. He hoped that the limousine was far enough down the street not to pay attention to his maneuver. He began to follow after the limousine, which was about three hundred feet ahead. The rules to this game had now changed. Kazinski was obviously forcing the girl to go alone in the limousine with him. Her safety became the uppermost concern.

Craig was edgy about investigating the warehouse on his own. He wasn't sure what he would find there, but he was certain that, whatever it was, it would not welcome him. He crept to the corner of the sheet metal fence and peered around to observe the warehouse's main entrance.

The warehouse took up the whole block running eastward to the next street. It was very run down. Its surrounding property was overgrown with straggly weeds that grew everywhere. There was the main entrance and then loading bays running eastward the whole length of the building. There were no windows in the structure. Everything was boarded-up. The front doors contained the only visible glass. The main part of the warehouse that contained the doors was made of solid red brick. Craig realized that the chances of being sighted by anybody who might be inside were minimal. Only someone outside would be able to easily see him approach, but there did not appear to be anyone outside on guard, nor did there seem to be anyone inside and behind the glass entrance doors. Craig considered his best move. He decided to walk farther east along Mill Street past the Canari Café. Once out of view of the front entrance on Cherry Street, he could cross onto the warehouse property and find a way in through one of the boarded-up loading bays.

He waited a moment before he made his move. He took a quick look around. There did not appear to be anyone in the vicinity. He hoped he was right. Craig came out from behind the fence and crossed Cherry Street in front of the café. He tried not to draw attention to himself. He walked along the north side of Mill Street and quickly out of the line of sight of the front of the warehouse. He stopped to reconnoiter.

Feeling that he was safe, he climbed through a hole that was in a section of the chain link fence that enclosed the warehouse just ahead. He was about fifty feet away from the loading bays and about a quarter of the way past the front entrance. Safely through the fence, he hurried over the property to the relative security of the loading bays. He rested a moment next to the building. He was in clear view from Mill Street and the café, but there was no one around to see him.

The loading bays were raised about three feet above the ground level. There were black rubber bumpers along the lower side to protect the bays from the trucks that once backed in there. He did not waste any time. He began to move westward to each of the boarded up loading bays leading towards the front of the warehouse. He was looking for a way in.

At the second bay he came to, there was a missing board and a hole that, upon examination, he discovered led into the warehouse. The hole was large enough for him to squeeze through. He took a quick look around and then drew out his revolver from inside his jacket holster with his right hand. Putting the gun forward he climbed up to the loading bay and stepped carefully through the hole and into the building.

The inside of the warehouse was lit by a row of yellowed fluorescent lights that went down the center of a long platform that ran the length of the warehouse. There were loading bays on both sides of the platform running the entire span of the building. There was no one to be seen anywhere near or on the platform.

Craig did not believe that the lights had been left on by mistake. Someone had to be inside the warehouse. He crouched down beside some old discolored cardboard boxes by the side of his loading bay and reconnoitered the inside of the building. It was now necessary to be even more cautious. Farther along the platform, he could make out the area that was adjacent to the front of the building. There was a two-story cinder block wall and a metal staircase with a platform that rose up from the center of the wall to what appeared to be an office on the second level. The door to the office was open and there was light coming from inside. The metal staircase was about twenty-five feet away from his present location.

In the other direction were more loading bays and the other end of the platform. Craig determined that the second level office was the only place that someone who was in the warehouse might be waiting. He decided to get closer and see what he could discover.

Carefully getting up, Craig moved closer. He used the empty boxes and skids to conceal himself as much as possible. He was cautious not to make any noise and kept his attention focused upon the office above. His gun was raised and pointed in the direction of the office.

He made his way to the metal staircase and hid underneath it. He had not yet spotted anyone. As he rested below the staircase, he began to hear the voices of men in casual conversation. The voices were coming from the office on the level above.

Craig nervously considered his next move. He did not like the idea of going blind into this situation. He would have preferred to have his partner with him, but that was not a possibility. He had to do something. He could not remain standing where he was for long, nor could he leave the warehouse without investigating further. He had to find out who or what was in the office above him. He had to go up the stairs.

Taking in a deep breath, he came from under the metal staircase and began to creep up the flight of stairs. He carefully stepped upon each metal step, using only the balls of his feet. He wanted to minimize any noise he might make going up the steps. The slightest creaking sound from the stairs might give him away He was beginning to perspire as he became more and more exposed upon the stairs. He realized that if he was heard by whoever was in the office and found on the stairs, he would be a sitting duck—and dead. It was imperative that he get quickly and quietly to the landing at the top of the stairs and take protection at the wall beside the office door. Once there he could better determine the number of men he was dealing with.

The sound of men talking inside the office continued, unaware of Craig's presence. Stepping as lightly as he could, he maneuvered his way up the stairs and onto the landing. He squeezed himself flat with his back against the wall. He was only inches away from the open office door. He could clearly hear the conversation from inside the office. He was perspiring and tense. Although he had been trained for such eventualities, he had never been in this type of situation before.

●

Inside the office, Kazinski's men were sitting about heatedly discussing something about gambling and the horses. They were oblivious to the fact that someone had found his way into the warehouse and was now standing just outside their door listening. Andrew was seated facing the open door. The two men were on either side of him. George was facing the bulletin board and the picture of the nude woman. Phil was facing across the room and out to the door. Both expected this to be an easy job that would soon be over. Neither man paid any attention to Andrew. As far as they were concerned, he was already dead.

●

Craig stood absolutely still. He had his gun raised and clutched in both hands. He was readying himself to go into 'the stance' and burst in on whoever was inside. He moved his right foot forward in preparation of his assault. In his apprehension, he did not see a loose bolt that was next to his right shoe. Inadvertently he kicked the bolt as he moved his foot and the bolt flew across the landing to the metal stairs where it noisily cascaded down. Craig froze in trepidation. The sound of the men talking inside the office instantly stopped. They were aware of his presence. He had just announced himself and lost his biggest element of surprise.

●

Phil and George abruptly stopped talking when they heard the noise on the stairs. In a reflex motion, they took out their guns and got to their feet. Someone was out on the stairs. They both silently communicated with each other through hand motions, and crept towards the office door. Andrew was full of apprehension. He was in open view in the center of the room directly in front of the office door.

●

Craig was at a loss. He had to make a move. The men inside were obviously alerted to his presence. He drew in a breath. All of his training came back to him. It was the only comfort he had. He went into an automated tactical response. With his gun out in front of him, he crouched down low, took a forceful step and barged into the office. It was his only remaining element of surprise.

"Ahhhhhhhhhhhhhhh!" he let out a cry as he leapt forward into the unknown.

●

Tom was able to keep the limousine in sight as it turned south on Parliament from Mill Street. It was still a good distance away from him. As it turned, he concluded that it was going back in the direction of the waterfront. He sped up trying to get a little closer. By the time he got to the corner of Mill Street and turned, the limousine was about two hundred feet south of him on Parliament crossing under the expressway and onto Queen's Quay. It was the way back to the waterfront and the hotel.

The limousine carried on along Queen's Quay and went out of sight around the curve of the road. Tom picked up speed. He knew this area well. He had to make the green light and not be forced to stop at the Expressway underpass. He wanted to keep the limousine in sight and not take any chances in losing them. Though he believed that the hotel was their destination, he could not be entirely certain. He decided not to call in. He wanted to wait 'til he actually followed them there and confirmed their location. It was very strange. He wondered why they were going back to the hotel.

Chapter 14

Monika was sitting nervously inside the limousine. Kazinski was on her right side. She was not sure what she should do. Time was running out. They were on Queen's Quay and almost at the hotel. She realized that as soon as Kazinski got the CDs from her at the hotel, both she and Andrew were dead. She had to find a way out of this mess, but she could not think of anything that she could do. She was not aware of Tom following after them. In her desperation she found herself thinking of James, wishing that he was here to help her. She missed him and was sorry that she had left him on such a sour note. She wanted to be away from all this and back safely with him. She racked her brains as the limousine pulled up into the drive of the hotel. She had to find a way out; a way to save herself and Andrew.

"I'll come with you just to make sure everything goes right." Kazinski suddenly spoke as the limousine stopped in front of the hotel main entrance. Monika was jarred from her thoughts.

The chauffeur got out and came back to the right passenger side of the limousine to open the door.

"Don't you trust me?" Monika was sarcastic.

"Let's just say that I do. That's why I'm coming."

Kazinski slid over and got out of the limousine. Once out he leaned back in and offered his hand to both help and control her movements.

Monika accepted his help. There was nothing else that she could do. She hoped an opportunity would reveal itself soon.

"Now don't try anything silly," Kazinski whispered into her ear as her head passed close to his. "Just get the CDs and we'll both come back and get into the car."

"Yeah," she reluctantly answered like a scolded school girl responding to a disciplinarian parent.

The hotel was very busy. A tour bus load of people pulled up and blocked the limousine in the drive while it began to unload its passengers. There was a lot of excited noise and commotion.

Kazinski took hold of Monika's right arm and

escorted her away from the chaos through the doors and into the lobby. It was also very busy inside the hotel. It appeared that an organization was arriving for a convention of some sort.

Kazinski and Monika crossed through the crowd and made their way to the front desk. They did not line up but went straight to an available clerk, which annoyed those who were waiting in line. Kazinski ignored their comments and pushed Monika forward to the counter.

"Yes, Ma'am." The clerk did not comment on their jumping the line, as he had recognized Kazinski. He did not wish to take any risks with one of the richest and most influential men in the city.

Monika took the receipt out of her purse and presented it to the clerk.

"I'm Monika Queller in 1711 South. I'd like to collect my package from safekeeping," she was tense as she spoke. Kazinski was right on top of her and there was nothing else she could say or do.

"Certainly, Ma'am." The clerk was very deferential as he took the receipt. "I'll get it right away."

The clerk turned and went through a door that led to the inner office behind, and out of sight of, the front desk area.

Monika remained standing tensely under the watchful eye of Kazinski.

"Very good. Once you get the CDs, we'll go back to the limousine," Kazinski spoke to her from behind. Though she had clearly heard him, she did not outwardly react.

Monika's heart was racing. Her mind was buzzing with all sorts of thoughts on what she should do after she got the package. She was almost at the wire and would have to do something before getting back into the limousine. She knew that she shouldn't get back into the limousine. If she did, she and Andrew would be 'dead meat'. She had do something and very soon—but what? Her desperation and panic were rising along with her heartbeat.

The commotion in the lobby area was increasing as the passengers from the newly-arrived tour bus outside entered the hotel. Monika turned her head and in a glance sized up the situation. She wasn't sure what she was going to do. She was acting on an instinct deep within her.

The clerk returned. Monika smiled at him and pretended that all was normal.

"Here you are, Ma'am." The clerk handed the package to her. He noted something strange about her and Kazinski, but said nothing about his observation. It was not his place to make such a comment.

"Thanks." She took the package. Both she and Kazinski turned and walked away from the counter.

"I'll take that." Kazinski tried to grab the envelope that contained the CDs from Monika on their way through the crowd of the lobby to the main entrance.

"No." She pulled the envelope away from Kazinski's attempt. "First you call and release Andrew." There was a pause between them. "Or I make a scene. Here and now," she threatened.

Kazinski did not want any trouble in such a public place. He grinned. He respected Monika's spunk.

"Okay. Fine," he accommodated her. "I'll call from the limousine."

They both made their way to the entrance and went through the revolving doors out onto the drive. The limousine was boxed in by the tour bus which was still unloading its passengers and their luggage. There was a chaotic crowd milling about, collecting belongings. The chauffeur was waiting at the limousine on the passenger side and opened the door. Monika got in first still clutching the envelope. Kazinski got in behind her. The door closed and the noise from outside was cut off. Monika's mind was spinning.

Why had she gotten back into the limousine? she chastised herself. It would be very difficult to get away once the limousine started moving.

The chauffeur went around to the front of the limousine and was looking for the driver of the tour bus to get him to hurry up and move the bus so that the limousine could get away.

"The CDs?" Kazinski asked.

"First the call," Monika was adamant.

Kazinski leaned over and picked up the phone that was hanging to his right beyond his door.

This was it. This was her opportunity. She could not wait any longer. It was now or never. She had to get out of the limousine and make a run for it. With Kazinski distracted, the chauffeur away, and the limousine boxed in, she had to make a move.

Keeping her eye on Kazinski who was beginning to punch in the phone number for the warehouse, she slid her hand onto the handle of her door. Once she felt its cool touch, she drew in a breath and strengthened her resolve to what she must do.

●

Tom had managed to catch up with the limousine as it pulled into the hotel driveway. He slowly followed behind and stopped to one side of the covered drive near the taxi stand not far from the main entrance. He had not been spotted. There was a lot of commotion in the drive and he felt safe remaining so close to Kazinski and Monika. They would not pay any attention to him in this chaos. A large tour bus pulled in after him and blocked any exit from the drive. Tom remained in the car and observed the limousine.

After a few moments the chauffeur got out and went to open the passenger door. Kazinski and

Monika got out. Monika seemed tense and afraid.

Tom watched through his windshield as they both entered into the hotel. He decided to get out and go into the lobby after them. He did not want to lose them.

●

Jeneau and James had made good time from the airport. They were now pulling onto the raised expressway and were about ten minutes from the hotel. Not far ahead of them were the skyscrapers of the downtown section and the buildings of the waterfront.

●

Tom took up position next to the main entrance just inside the lobby. The crowd made it difficult for him to see Kazinski and Monika, but he managed to keep them in sight as they crossed over to the front desk. He saw Monika talking to the clerk. Then the clerk went away and, after several moments, returned with a Kraft envelope which he gave to her. Kazinski was very close behind her. They both walked away from the counter. Kazinski tried to forcefully take the envelope from her. Clearly, Monika was in distress. Tom wondered what might be in the envelope that Kazinski wanted so badly.

As they came back to the entrance, Tom noted the strain on Monika's face. She seemed to be in the midst of a great dilemma, though she did not seem to be in any immediate danger. He did not intervene. He acted as if he was waiting for some-one. His orders were clear. He was to follow them and keep them in sight. He was not to interfere unless there was an obvious threat to her well-being.

Kazinski and Monika passed in front of him. They paid him no attention as they passed through the doors together en route to the limousine. Outside upon seeing them return, the chauffeur opened the passenger door.

They were going to leave. Tom hurried out of the lobby through the revolving glass doors, and crossed back to his car.

●

Monika silently prepared herself. On the count of three she decided to make her move. It was her only hope. It really was now or never. She want-ed to at least go down fighting. If she could get away, she might be able to save Andrew and her-self. Kazinski would do no harm to either of them as long as he did not have the CDs. She began to count to herself. One....Two...Three!

On three she tensed the muscles of her arm along to her hand and in one swift movement, opened the door to her left side and made her dar-ing escape.

Kazinski was caught completely off-guard. He had never anticipated this reaction from Monika.

"Jesus!" he exclaimed after her. He had made a terrible mistake. He hung up the phone and scrambled to get out of the limousine.

Monika was getting away through the crowd that had just gotten off the tour bus. She was headed out from the hotel to Queen's Quay.

"Austin!" He tried to get the chauffeur's attention. "Austin!"

The chauffeur responded to Kazinski's call. He broke off his discussion with the tour bus driver and turned to his employer's voice. Kazinski indicated through hand signals: 'Over there. OVER THERE!'

The chauffeur followed the signals and saw Monika running down the drive of the hotel. He understood. She was getting away and Kazinski wanted him to help stop her.

Monika had made it out of the limousine and was headed anywhere as far away from Kazinski as possible. She realized that she needed a better means of escape than on foot. As she ran along the drive, she came upon the golf cart that the bell hops used to carry luggage and patrons from Queen's Quay up the steep driveway into the hotel. The cart was unattended. She jumped into it. She was lucky. The keys were in the ignition. She pushed the pedal with her right foot and the electric cart sprang forward with a whine. She drove down the drive and turned left onto Queen's Quay. She was not sure where she was going. She just wanted to get away as fast as she could.

Both Kazinski and his chauffeur watched

Monika's get-away from the hotel driveway onto the main street in shock. There was no time to waste. Kazinski ran to the driver's door and got in behind the steering wheel of the limousine. He slammed the limousine into gear and started forward honking the horn and swearing at the people that were in his way; this slowed his progress and inadvertently helped Monika to get away. Getting nowhere on the drive, he drove up onto the sidewalk along the hotel entrance to get around the parked tour bus. Pandemonium ensued. There were screams as people started running chaotically to get out of the way of the limousine and its maniacal driver.

●

Tom was as surprised as everyone else by the events that unfolded after Monika opened the limousine door and ran out. He saw her get into the cart and drive off. He realized that she was getting away not only from Kazinski, but also from him. He got back into his car and tried to follow the limousine, but the crowd was too thick. He was forced to stop and watch helplessly as Kazinski, in the limousine, made his way along the sidewalk and out of the hotel drive onto Queen's Quay after Monika.

Tom picked up the phone in his car and punched in Jeneau's cellular number. Tom became frustrated as the phone rang and Jeneau didn't pick up right away.

"Come on. Where are you?"

●

Jeneau picked up the phone after four rings. He and James were just exiting from the expressway and the traffic off the expressway onto the ramp prevented him from picking up the phone right away.

"Jeneau." He finally spoke into the phone as he drove from the ramp past Lakeshore Boulevard to Queen's Quay West. They were only a mile or so from the hotel.

" ....
....
............................."

'Golf cart?" Jeneau's expression became strained. "Don't worry. We're on it." He hung up.

"What's up?" James was worried.

"Look for a golf cart. Your girlfriend's just made a break from Kazinski and needs our help."

●

By the time Kazinski made it to the street, Monika was a block away on Queen's Quay traveling west. She kept looking behind her to see if she was being followed. She swerved in and out around the cars that were in her way. The sight of the golf cart hurrying along the road drew a lot of attention. When she spotted the limousine coming out from the hotel driveway, she panicked. She had a good lead but the golf cart was not fast enough to get away from the limousine. Monika decided to turn up the first street she came to in an effort to evade the limousine.

●

"There. Over there!" James spotted the golf cart as it turned up the street which led to the CN Tower. He was happy to see that Monika was alive, but he felt a sense of urgency set in.

"Hurry," was all he could say.

●

Kazinski saw the cart ahead. He watched as it turned up a street and moved out of sight. He pushed on the gas and sped along the roadway, weaving in and out of the cars that got in his way. He ran through a red light and almost hit a car that was going southbound onto Queen's Quay. The car swerved and honked at the limousine as it continued along in its pursuit of the cart.

The limousine came to the street that Monika had taken. Kazinski again spotted the cart. It was ahead and almost at the access road to the CN Tower and the domed stadium. She was within his grasp again. He sped up to close the gap. She had gone up a road that had no exit. She would be trapped.

Monika was in a panic. The limousine was gaining on her. She came to the entry road to the Tower and the domed stadium. She slowed the cart trying to decide what she should do. Kazinski was not far behind her. The road continued left and right around the buildings. She knew that she could not outrun the limousine on the roadway. She had to do something else.

She focused her attention on the space ahead of her beyond the roadway. There was a large fountain and a promenade between the stadium and the Tower. The area was not very busy. She could drive the cart across the promenade and get to the Tower. It was her only hope.

Monika drove up over the curb from the road and onto the promenade. The limousine was still gaining on her. She pushed the accelerator as far as it would go, but the cart was running out of electrical power and would not go any faster. She headed for the base of the colossal Tower that floated overhead. She hoped that she could make it into the Tower and lose Kazinski amongst the crowd of tourists that she assumed would be inside.

●

Jeneau and James came to the intersection about fifteen seconds after the limousine had recklessly followed the cart from Queen's Quay onto the road, towards the Tower. They both noted the vehicle because of the manner in which it was driving and instantly put it together with the escaping cart only a few seconds before. They both looked to each other and said in unison:

"Kazinski."

"Let's go." James brightened. He didn't want to lose Monika now. Not when he and Jeneau were so close to helping her. If only there was a way to let her know he was here and that she was not alone. But there wasn't.

The rear tires on Jeneau's car squealed as he turned the corner and sped after the limousine. Kazinski had a very small lead on them. Jeneau wanted to get to Kazinski before he caught up with the cart and Monika. Both Jeneau and James knew what Kazinski would do if he got to Monika first.

●

The few people who were either walking on the promenade or sitting by the large fountain to the west of the Tower were not very alarmed by the cart pulling onto the sidewalk and traveling on the promenade in the direction of the Tower. It was not unusual for the grounds keepers to use vehicles like the cart to get around and maintain the property. The only unusual thing was the speed with which it sped along the promenade; a speed that some of the people did not appreciate and caused them to peer and some to yell out after Monika: 'slow down!'

Monika did not care about their admonishments. She was almost at the base of Tower, close to the entrance. The Tower was directly over top. Its grey triangular stick-like cement trunk dove deep into the promenade and held up the circular pod eleven hundred feet above. Monika was overwhelmed by its grand size and proportions. From a distance she had thought the structure more delicate as it pierced like a needle through the skyline and floated amongst the clouds of Emerald City. Up close, it was very big, grey and solid — not at all needle-like.

There was an elevator moving down the center of the cement pillar of the Tower behind a glassed-in channel that she had not noticed before. Below the channel, just ahead of her where the Tower connected to the ground, there was an entrance.

Monika steered in the direction of the entrance. She checked behind her quickly to see if she could make it there safely before the limousine. She saw the limousine. It was still gaining on her. It had come to the end of the road, but it did not stop. As it came to the promenade, it drove up over the curb like Monika had done with the golf cart, and continued to pick up speed on the promenade behind.

A large black limousine speeding along the promenade caused an outcry from the pedestrians. They screamed and yelled as those in the path of the vehicle got out of its way. Monika realized that whoever was driving the limousine was very determined to catch up with her and nothing would stop him.

Monika drove the remaining few feet and arrived at the Tower entrance. The limousine was almost upon her. She took her foot off the accelerator pedal and the cart slowed. She did not wait for the cart to completely stop. She jumped from it and ran up to the glass entry doors of the Tower. She opened one of the two doors and ran inside. As she entered into the Tower, the limousine came to a stop next to the cart and Kazinski got out to chase after her.

Inside, Monika found a large room. There were gift shops, a refreshment stand and a place to buy tickets to ride the elevator up to the top of the Tower. There was a crowd of people in the area and a small group of older women tourists standing together and waiting to get on the elevator. The women were listening to their young male tour guide who was helping them onto the elevator and talking about the Tower. Monika moved over and stood just next to the elevator and the group. She looked a little frazzled. She was not certain what she should do or where she should hide. With her back to the wall, she watched for Kazinski and his men. They would be here any second. She considered her options.

"Come on dear." An older woman who was part of the tourist group and standing next to Monika took her arm and broke her from her concentration.

The woman was short and matronly. She must have been in her early seventies and reminded Monika of her grandmother. The woman dragged her along and onto the elevator with the rest of her group.

"There's room for you with us. If you don't mind riding with a bunch of old cronies." The woman smiled.

"Oh... No... Not at all." Monika wasn't sure what to do. She went along and stood concealed on the elevator amongst these women. She half listened and spoke to them while she kept the other half of her attention on the main entrance.

"So where are you from?" The older woman was very conversational.

"Oceanside... San Francisco originally."

As she spoke, Monika saw Kazinski come through the entrance. He stopped and reconnoitered. Monika tried to duck amongst the woman.

"What's wrong dear?" the older woman asked after seeing Monika's strange behavior.

"Oh... Ah... Nothing...I..."

"Man trouble." The older woman interrupted. She looked out of the elevator's open doors and saw Kazinski standing and searching. She put it all together. "Tell me about it. Don't worry. Make him chase you a little. I used to give my Fred the hardest time. But it kept him attentive." She smiled.

Monika nodded but was distant as she watched after Kazinski. She tried to conceal herself from his view.

"When do we go?" Monika nervously blurted out loud trying to prompt the tour guide to close the elevator doors and begin the climb to the top.

As if it was the cue that he was waiting for, the tour guide pushed a button and the elevator doors began to close. Monika felt relieved.

●

Kazinski was out of breath. He stood checking through the crowd of people inside the building, but he was unable to locate Monika. Just as the elevator doors were closing, he saw her. She was in the elevator going to the top of the Tower. Their eyes met as the doors closed and she went out of sight. He hurried over to the elevator. There was a sign attached to the wall beside the closed elevator doors: 'OBSERVATION DECK'. There was a Tower employee standing beside the elevator.

"When's the next elevator to the deck?" Kazinski asked.

"Any time now, but you need a ticket."

"Where do I get the ticket?"

"Over there." The employee indicated the ticket booth a few feet away.

"Thanks."

Kazinski crossed over to the ticket booth and got in line. There were two people in front of him and he was becoming agitated that he might miss the next elevator. He kept turning his head to check for the elevator.

The two people in front of him quickly bought their tickets and got out of the way. It was Kazinski's turn. He came up to the window. There was a young girl waiting to take his request.

"One." Kazinski demanded.

"Eight dollars please, sir."

He rifled though his pants left pocket and removed a few bills. He examined them quickly and handed her two blue ones.

The girl took the money and made change, giving him the ticket with the change.

"Thank you," she said.

Kazinski took the ticket and nodded his acknowledgment of her thanks. He turned and went back to the elevator. There were about ten people waiting for the next ride up to the deck.

●

The view from the ride up the Tower was inspiring. Monika was able to see the complete southwest area of the city and lake through the twilight of the summer evening. There was a least an hour left of dusk. The setting sun glittered off the lake which, from the vantage of the Tower, was clearly more like an ocean in size than a lake. She relaxed a little in the security of the group of women and the safety of the elevator.

When they arrived at the observation deck, Monika parted company with the group. The realization that Kazinski was not far behind sank in. She walked out onto the deck that went three hundred and sixty degrees around the Tower.

The Deck was enclosed and comprised of two sections. There was an interior section protected from the outside by glass windows and an outer section that was exposed to the elements. The only barrier between the outer deck and the sky was a metal cage that enclosed the perimeter. Though it appeared solid, Monika did not want to go out there.

She began to walk around the deck looking for someplace to hide from Kazinski. He would certainly come up and look for her. If she could fool him into believing that she had somehow gotten past him and taken another elevator down, then she would be okay. She hoped that he would then go back down the Tower. This would allow her to get away and find help. The CDs were in her purse. She needed to keep Kazinski from getting them, at least until she could assure Andrew's safety.

About half-way around the deck Monika came to a door that led out from the deck. She opened it and found herself on the outer deck next to a small barricade. There was a large sign attached to the barricade. The writing was very bold and written in red paint. The thought of what danger lurked beyond the barricade sent a chill up her spine:

DANGER
THIS SECTION CLOSED TO PUBLIC
FOR REPAIRS

This was the ideal place to hide. There was no one near to see her. She climbed over the barricade.

On the other side of the barricade, it was very windy. The cage to the outer deck was dismantled in one of its sections. There was a large hole exposed to the sky. There were several large metal cylinders which she assumed were used by the workers to weld and repair the metal of the cage. She carefully crossed over to the cylinders and wedged herself behind them. She crouched down and sat on the floor with her back to the cement wall of the Tower and waited. It was cold and uncomfortable. She hoped it would soon be over.

●

Jeneau and James had followed after the limousine and Monika's cart. They saw Monika get out of the cart and run into the Tower. They also watched as Kazinski came to the Tower and followed along only twenty or so seconds behind her. They were about the same distance behind Kazinski. He was just far enough ahead of them to get away.

By the time they arrived at the base of the Tower, after having crossed over the promenade and entering into the building, Monika and Kazinski had disappeared. Jeneau and James both stood inside the front entrance searching for either of them.

"Where'd they go?" Jeneau questioned out loud.

Before them was the large open space of the

Tower gift shops, refreshment stands, elevators and ticket booth. There were quite a few tourists milling about or just waiting for the elevators.

"You look down here, and I'll go to the top." James urgently needed to find Monika. She was in danger. They could find her faster by splitting up.

"Okay." Jeneau agreed "Will you be able to identify him?"

"Yes." James' skill as an agent was remarkable. The glimpse that he had caught of Kazinski, as he exited from the limousine on the promenade en route to the Tower, was enough for him to recall the man in detail. He would have no problem picking him out of any crowd.

"Do you have a weapon?"

"No."

"Here. Take mine." Jeneau reached his hand under his coat and presented a small revolver to him. He noted James' surprise at the size of the gun.

"It's my spare." Jeneau smiled.

"Thanks." James took the tiny revolver.

They separated. Jeneau went into the crowd and the shops; James crossed over to the elevator to catch the next ride up. Another elevator was just arriving. James quickened his pace. He did not need a ticket. He would use the power of his badge.

●

Kazinski arrived about a minute after Monika on the observation deck. The crowd in the elevator pushed out onto the inner deck. He found his way and stood about five feet away from the elevator doors, examining the area. The deck was not as crowded as he had expected for this time of year. The people were scattered throughout the inner and exterior sections. He carefully checked through the people on this section of the three hundred and sixty degree observation deck. Monika was nowhere to be seen. He studied the deck. The dusk sky was a beautiful purple and pink color. The sun was beginning to set.

"So where are you hiding?" He spoke to himself as he tried to imagine where she might have gone.

He turned and started to walk counter-clockwise. As he walked, he searched for a possible escape route or hiding place. He came to the same door that Monika had just gone through a few minutes before. He paused at the door and then tried the handle. It opened. He went out onto the outer deck.

It was cool on the outer deck. There was a fairly strong wind blowing. Kazinski turned up the lapels of his jacket to keep warm. He looked around. To his left was a tall barricade with a sign that warned of danger, closing that section off to the public. Kazinski looked out through the open part of the section.

There was no one out here, and he was feeling

the cold. He decided to go back into the interior section and search there before he wasted too much time out here. He was concerned that Monika may be ahead of him on the inner deck and rounding to the elevators. He turned, re-opened the door and went back to the interior deck.

●

Monika was tense. She heard the door that led to the interior deck open and the sound of footsteps upon the concrete floor. The steps came towards the barrier a few feet away from her and stopped. There was silence. Monika began to shiver both with the cold and her own nervousness. She held her breath and waited, straining her ears for any sound above the wind. She felt an evil presence. Then the footsteps started again. She began to panic. She heard the door open and the steps continued until the door slammed shut. There was silence. She was alone and trapped. She remained in her hiding place behind the cylinders and hoped that if the footsteps had been Kazinski's, he would not come back.

●

James arrived shortly after Kazinski on the observation deck. He was anxious to start his search of the deck. He separated himself from the crowd coming off the elevator, turned left along the interior deck and started to work his way round counter-clockwise.

●

Kazinski had gone round the deck and was now back at the elevator. Although he had come across many people, not one of them had been Monika. Nor had he seen any place that she could be hiding. He had tried every door that he had come to and the only ones that opened were the ones that led to the outer deck.

He stood mystified at the elevator considering where Monika might have gone. He did not believe that she had taken another elevator down. He just believed that she was here hiding somewhere. The only place that he had not searched was the area of the outer deck that was closed for repair. He decided to go back to that section and investigate beyond the barricade.

●

James did not realize how close he was to both Kazinski or Monika. He had carefully been going around the deck and was only forty or so feet behind Kazinski, but in another quadrant of the circular inner deck. He was rushing along and becoming frustrated at not finding them.

'Where could they have gone?' he thought to himself. 'If they had come up here, there was no way that either of them would have been able to get by and down the elevator.'

He decided to continue on around and, if he didn't find them, then he would go back down and check with Jeneau. Some instinct inside him told him that he was on the correct path; that Monika and Kazinski were both very near. He felt their presence. He continued walking.

●

As James walked, so did Kazinski. If he had stopped five seconds longer, James would have come into his quadrant and spied him. Kazinski was unconcerned about being chased himself. He was unaware of James or his possible presence. He did not know that Monika had already unwittingly sent out an alert. As it happened, he started moving forward in search of her and by chance kept out of James' view.

Kazinski hurried over to the door that led to the outer deck and the barricaded section. He put his hand upon the door handle and opened it.

●

Again Monika heard the door open and footsteps walking toward the barricade. It had only been a couple of minutes since it had last been opened. Her instincts and senses heightened. She heard the same steps stop at the barricade and then a rattling sound as someone started to climb, as she had done, over the barrier.

She pushed herself back against the wall as far as she could and peeked through a crack towards the barrier. After a few moments she saw a man— it was Kazinski, climbing over the top of the barricade and jumping onto her side of the restricted deck. She was so nervous that she could not stop herself from shaking. Her breathing became short. She was panting like a cornered animal trying to evade its capture or death. Adrenaline was pumping solidly through her veins. She felt afraid but strangely elated as she awaited his discovery of her. She grabbed onto her purse for reassurance and prepared herself.

●

Kazinski was not in good physical condition. He had difficulty climbing over the barricade and into the restricted section of the deck. He was very clumsy and noisy in his climb. Once on the other side, he brushed himself off and then began to investigate the section.

A little ways in front of him was a broken section of the metal cage of the outer deck. It was about four feet large and exposed to the sky. He regarded the opening from his position and winced at the distance to the ground and domed stadium below. It was a long way down to the ground below. The people on the promenade looked like ants as they walked across the open area at ground level. A chill of fear of the height ran up his spine. He would be pleased to get back down to ground level. He brought his attention back to the outer deck.

"Ms. Queller. I know you're here. Why don't you come and give me the CDs?" He did not know that she was there. He was just playing a hunch. Maybe he could fake her out.

"You've got nowhere to go and you can't stay up here indefinitely." He walked slowly forward as he spoke, and stopped in front of the cylinders.

Monika was stunned. She wondered if he really knew that she was hiding there or was just trying to fool her. From the tone of his voice, she did not get the feeling that Kazinski really was aware of her hiding place, but she was not certain.

"Come on Monika. Let's get this over with. You know that you can't hide from me forever." He was still standing in front of her hiding place, but had not seen her tucked in behind the cylinders.

Monika could see him through the crack between two of the cylinders. She squeezed herself in tighter to conceal herself. In doing so she caused one of the cylinders to move. It was a very slight movement accompanied by a short scrapping sound against the cement wall.

Kazinski instantly focused on the source of the noise. He realized that there was only one reason for the cylinder to move—Monika had to be hiding behind the cylinders. He put his hand into his jacket and pulled out a gun. He moved closer to the cylinders and began to search for her.

"I know you're there." He spoke with confidence. "Come out. Now." He raised his gun and aimed it into the area of the cylinders.

Monika could see that he was pointing the weapon directly at her position. There was nothing she could do but comply.

"Okay. Don't shoot. I'm coming out," she called out loudly from behind the cylinders.

Kazinski was pleased that his ploy had worked. He readied himself for her appearance.

"No tricks now, Ms. Queller. Nice and easy. Keep your hands in view if you don't mind." He was acting charming again.

Monika pulled herself up and stood facing Kazinski.

"There. I told you you couldn't hide from me. Now where is the envelope with the disks?"

"In my purse." Monika had her arms in front of her and raised half way up. She indicated with a tilting of her head the purse that hung over her shoulder on her left side.

"Slowly take it off and throw it to me. SLOW-LY." He threatened her with the gun.

Monika was trapped. She did not want to give him the purse with the CDs, but there seemed to be nothing else that she could do.

Slowly she moved her arms and, using her right hand, carefully removed the strap that held the purse off of her shoulder. The purse slowly slid down. She held the purse out in front of her and offered it to him.

"Put it down there and walk over to the opening," he ordered. He would take the CDs and then get rid of Monika. He would force her through the hole in the cage where she would fall to her death. It was very convenient. It would be called an accident.

Monika realized at that moment what Kazinski was planning.

"What are you going to do?" she asked as she still held the purse.

"You're going to have a fall. A long fall." He smiled at her. "Put the purse down and move." He was more forceful and threatening with the gun.

Monika understood. It was either be shot or fall. Neither option satisfied her. Slowly she moved the purse away from her towards the floor. She had to try something—but what? She realized that the CDs were of the utmost importance to Kazinski and that he would do nothing to her as long as she held onto the CDs. She could not meekly give in to him. As the purse was lowered, she mustered the courage for what might be her one last chance.

●

James had done a complete search of the interior of the observation deck and had stopped next to the door that led to the outer deck and the closed off section. He was afraid. He wasn't sure what had happened to Monika or Kazinski. This was the last place that he could check for them. He went to the door and exited onto the outer deck.

●

Suddenly the wind in the deck changed its strength and made a whining sound as the door that separated inside from out was opened and broke the vacuum of the inner deck. This was the opportunity that Monika needed to act.

Upon hearing the door open, Kazinski's attention was momentarily distracted away from Monika. He turned his head to quickly check behind him and then swung back to Monika. During that split second, Monika took the purse and flung it towards the hole in the cage and then ducked for cover. The purse headed for the hole. Time seemed to slow as the purse flew through the air towards the opening.

"NO!" Kazinski lowered his gun and made a dive in the direction of the purse.

The purse went through the hole and, just when all seemed lost, its strap caught on a piece of the metal bars of the cage at the opening. The purse stopped its journey and hung precariously from the strap, swaying in the wind.

●

James entered the outer deck and stopped in front of the barricade. He heard a cry as he read the warning sign. It came from behind the barricaded section of the deck. Without hesitating he knew that he had found them and ran forward, drawing his gun and scrambling over the barricade. From the sound of the cry, there was no time to waste.

●

Kazinski climbed out onto the cage. The cage jutted out from the cement ledge of the outer deck and rose up at a forty degree angle where, about fifteen feet out from the Tower, it attached to the cement floor of the protruding floor above. Stepping out onto the cage, there was nothing but the inch thick intertwined metal bars holding him above the cement promenade eleven hundred feet below. It was an eerie sensation. It almost made him feel like he was weightless and floating in the atmosphere. He climbed out along the cage to the opening.

The cage at this point had been partially dismantled and a few of the cross bars were showing signs of fatigue. The metal cage squeaked under the sudden additional weight that was being placed upon it at its weakest point near the hole. Until the hole was fixed and new bars welded into place, the whole area was not reliable to support any extra weight.

Kazinski ignored the sounds of the cage as it strained and shifted. The strap of the purse was beginning to slip off the bar that held it as he came closer to the hole.

Monika took advantage of Kazinski's foolhardy choice to go after the purse and headed for the barricade, away from Kazinski. She knew that she had to get back to the elevator before he retrieved the purse and came after her.

As she crossed to the barricade, she was startled to see James flying over it and landing hard on his feet on the cement floor.

"JAMES?!" Monika exclaimed. She was about to question him further, but she was so relieved that he was here, and that she would now be safe from Kazinski, that she ran to him and hugged and kissed him. She was in tears as she spoke.

"Oh James. How?... When?... Why?..." she was kissing him as she blurted out the words.

"Are you okay?" James returned her kisses.

"Yes." Monika sagged with relief against him.

There was no time to spend on long explanations or greetings. James pulled Monika away from him and placed her in safety behind him. He drew his gun and yelled out to Kazinski, who was paying no attention to them as he stretched out for the strap of the purse.

"Kazinski!" James shouted out to him. "It's over."

Kazinski became aware of James. He looked back and propped himself up at the opening next to the purse. He did not speak. He aimed his gun at James and was about to shoot. Nothing was going to stop him now. There was nothing left to lose.

James could see down the barrel of Kazinski's gun as it pointed directly at him. In the split seconds that passed he saw Kazinski's forefinger beginning to squeeze the trigger. There was no time to think. James relied on his instincts. He pushed Monika away. There were no other options left to him. James fired.

The shot hit Kazinski in the left shoulder. The force of the bullet at such close quarters pushed him back. Kazinski dropped his gun. It hit the metal cage then slipped out into the open vastness. He brought his right arm around and clasped at the wound. Blood covered his hand. He had an astonished look upon his face. He fell back against the weakened bars. The bars gave way and he tumbled out.

Somehow Kazinski had managed to grab hold of a part of the cage with his left hand as he fell. He screamed out in pain and fear.

"Help me! Please. Help me!"

James ran over to the cage and considered what he could do. The part of the cage near to him appeared secure. He might be able to distribute his weight and reach out and try to grab hold of Kazinski's hand.

"Hurry. I can't hold on." Kazinski pleaded. His shoulder was in terrible pain and his grip upon the metal bar of the cage was slipping. He was dangling eleven hundred feet above the ground. The motion of his swinging made it even harder for him to hold on.

"Hold on. I'm coming. You can do it." James decided to start out onto the cage and help. He had to. He could not let Kazinski fall to his death.

"James?!" Monika was horrified by what James was about to attempt. The cage did not look strong enough around the hole to support both

Kazinski and him.

"Don't worry." James turned and smiled. "I love you."

Monika was frozen to the spot with apprehension as James climbed out onto the cage.

The cage squeaked and shifted which scared both James and Monika. Monika gasped. James stopped.

"Hurry up!" Kazinski pleaded. He could not hold on much longer.

James stretched out his right arm and grabbed for Kazinski's hand upon the bar. He was not that far away.

"Hurry. I can't...ho...hol." Kazinski let go just as James grabbed onto his wrist. The strain on James of the sudden weight of Kazinski made him groan.

"Use your other hand. Grab on!" James did not have a good grasp. He felt Kazinski slipping away.

"Grab my hand!" Their eyes met.

James tried to hold on. He extended every bit of strength he could muster, but Kazinski was slipping through his hand.

"Grab on!"

"I can't."

"Grab on. Use your other hand!"

Kazinski attempted to bring his arm up. He managed to grab onto James' hand, but could not get a good grip. The blood from his wound was covering his palm and was causing him to slip from James' hand. He needed to grab on above James' wrist.

"Grab on! Higher." James continued to encourage. There was not much of a grip left.

Suddenly Kazinski slipped from James. There was a last stare of fear and desperation as Kazinski began to free-fall through the air. Kazinski let out a horrified squeal. There would not be much left of him after he hit the ground below.

James closed his eyes and shook his head in dismay. He had come so close but just could not hold him.

Monika brought her hands up and covered her mouth as Kazinski's scream became more distant.

"Oh no!" she gasped. The thought of such an abysmal fate horrified her.

Chapter 15

FOUR DAYS LATER

The elevator opened on the ground floor. Monika and James walked out and into the lobby of the Weston Hotel. They were leaving for home on the morning flight. They went into the main lobby past the front desk. Jeneau was there waiting for them. James was carrying Monika's bag.

"Are you sure I can't get you two to stay any longer? It's on us." Jeneau greeted them and spoke to James as they approached.

"No. It's time we got back home." James presented his hand to Jeneau.

"Monika?" Jeneau dipped his head in deference to her and smiled.

He had only known these two for a few short

days, but he had come to like them a lot. They made a nice couple.

"No we can't. There's lots to plan." Monika flashed her left hand at him. On her fourth finger was the engagement ring that James had brought with him for her.

"Don't forget to send me an invitation." He leaned over and kissed her hand. "I know you will both be very happy."

"What about Andrew?" Monika changed the subject as they all crossed through the lobby to the front entrance. She had visited him in hospital over the past few days, and though he was recovering from his ordeal, she was still very concerned about him. They had become very attached—like family. He was now like a brother to her.

"Andrew is recovering fine. He will soon be as good as new. He wanted me to thank you again, for everything."

"I'm glad he's okay. Remind him that I expect to see him soon. He'll be getting an invitation too."

"I will."

"And my purse?"

"We have not been able to find it, but we will keep looking. The information on the CDs will be useless to ABM now. With Kazinski gone and their activities exposed they will have many difficulties ahead."

"It's hard to believe that they got away with it for so long."

"Yes. But that's all over now. If it hadn't been for you…" Jeneau did not need to finish the sentence. They all understood.

"The least you both can do, then, is allow me to drive you to the airport."

"Deal." Monika offered her hand and grinned as they shook. She was happy that she and James had found this new friend. Everything had worked out for the best.

After a moment's pause, they continued on across the lobby. There was nothing more to be said. They came to the revolving doors of the hotel entrance. Monika went first, then James, followed by Jeneau. They all exited through to the hotel driveway and Jeneau's car.

TWO WEEKS LATER

•

The sound of modems connecting can be heard in a darkened room. Gradually the light of a computer monitor comes into view. Upon the screen can be seen dialogue boxes as the modem is connecting and then downloading data from another computer. The other computer is in a federal department in Washington DC. There has been no security alert or password requested. It has been a very easy and straight forward operation. The computer is connected without problems and begins to give up its secrets…again.

•